The Secret of
Sarah Revere

*Other Great Episodes
by Ann Rinaldi*

AN ACQUAINTANCE WITH DARKNESS

A BREAK WITH CHARITY
A Story about the Salem Witch Trials

CAST TWO SHADOWS
The American Revolution in the South

THE FIFTH OF MARCH
A Story of the Boston Massacre

FINISHING BECCA
*A Story about Peggy Shippen and
Benedict Arnold*

HANG A THOUSAND TREES WITH RIBBONS
The Story of Phillis Wheatley

A RIDE INTO MORNING
The Story of Tempe Wick

The Secret of

Sarah Revere

A N N   R I N A L D I

Gulliver Books/Harcourt, Inc.

San Diego   *New York*   *London*

Requests for permission to make copies of any part of
the work should be mailed to the following address:
Permissions Department, Harcourt, Inc.,
6277 Sea Harbor Drive, Orlando, Florida 32887-6777.

Gulliver Books is a registered trademark of Harcourt, Inc.

Library of Congress Cataloging-in-Publication Data
Rinaldi, Ann.
The secret of Sarah Revere/Ann Rinaldi.
p.   cm.
"Gulliver Books."
Includes bibliographical references.
Summary: Paul Revere's daughter describes her father's "rides" and
the intelligence network of the patriot community prior to the
American Revolution.
1. Revere, Paul, 1735–1818—Juvenile fiction. [1. Revere, Paul.
1735–1818—Fiction. 2. Spies—Fiction. 3. Silversmiths—Fiction.
4. Fathers and daughters—Fiction. 5. United States—History—
Revolution, 1775–1783—Fiction.] I. Title.
PZ7.R49Se 1995
[Fic]—dc20 95-5570
ISBN 0-15-200393-2 ISBN 0-15-200392-4 (pb)

Text set in Bulmer
Designed by Kaelin Chappell
M L K J I H G F E D
R Q P O N M L K J   (pb)
Printed in the United States of America

For my son, Ron,

and others like him,
who remember our history
with the pride our
Founding Fathers meant us
all to have

Listen, my children, and you shall hear
Of the midnight ride of Paul Revere,
On the eighteenth of April, in Seventy-five;
Hardly a man is now alive
Who remembers that famous day and year.

From "Paul Revere's Ride"
Henry Wadsworth Longfellow
April 1860

Acknowledgments

I WISH TO THANK the staff of the Paul Revere House at 19 North Square in Boston's North End for their kindness and assistance.

The mere fact that this house still exists, that it has survived three hundred years of our history (it was originally built in 1680), is a miracle in itself. It was a rooming house in the nineteenth century, when that part of Boston was an immigrant slum.

In 1902, it was purchased by one of Revere's great-grandsons and, within a few years, restored by the Paul Revere Memorial Association, opening its doors to the public as one of the first historic house museums in the country in 1908.

All who consider themselves Americans should be grateful to everyone who had a hand in preserving it.

Appreciation goes to the writers of the academic books I used for my research, and to my editor, Karen Grove, who is always receptive to a new idea.

And thanks, once again, to my son, Ron, whose interest in history rallied me to write historical novels, as surely as Paul Revere rallied the inhabitants of so many New England towns with his cry of "The Regulars are coming!"

Watertown

Chapter One

17 • JUNE • 1775

*T*HAT MAN is at the gate again. For the second time this day. You would think that with all that is going on, he would have the sense to stay away.

The air is so hot. Nothing bestirs. And the only sound comes from the guns on the hill. Sometimes it stops. The silence is worse.

People come out of their houses to look. At what? If we were in Boston we could at least *see* what is going on. But here, seven miles up the Charles from Boston, we cannot.

Then the guns start again, like thunder. Oh, I wish it were thunder! We need rain.

Is that man going to come through the gate? Or just stand there? I've closed all the shutters so he'll think we're sleeping. Look at him, ruffles at his throat, wearing black broadcloth like it was December in Boston. A minister, he says. Some man of God, that he isn't sensible of the troubles we all have in Watertown this day.

I *told* him before that baby Joshua kept us up all night. And that Father is busy. Why doesn't he go away? How to be rid of him?

Rachel. No, I can't bother Rachel. She needs her sleep. Grandmother? *She* could scare him off. She could scare the British off the hill. They should have let her go and fight them. She's gone to market. No more sickness in her bones. She's come to life in Watertown. All the prominent Whigs are here. Anyway, I've never asked her for help and I'll not start now.

Where is everyone else who lives in this house?

Oh yes, the Knoxes went out. Mr. Knox said something about helping to build fortifications. Can't wait to get himself killed, it seems. Married only a year and they sneaked out of Boston with his sword hidden under her skirts, soon as the fighting started, so he could be in on it.

Where did his wife, Lucy, go? To Betsy Hunt

Palmer's to make ready lint and linen. My sister Debby is with her. Well, at least they took the children. There's a blessing.

Lint and linen for the wounded. Doctor Warren thought to ask them to do that.

No, don't think of Doctor Warren.

But I must think of him. I have been unable to think of anything else in the near six weeks that we have been here.

I have a score to settle with Doctor Warren. And he has one to settle with me. A matter lies between us, as disturbing in my mind as the matter that lies between the colonials and the British.

But there has been no time to resolve it. And I ache inside, thinking that perhaps the time for settling it has come and gone. That one gets only so many chances to make things right with another human being. And then it is too late.

He has not been around much, for one thing. Since the twenty-second of April he has been too busy. Making an army. Father said Warren did that, went right to Cambridge with the militia as soon as they got done chasing Lord Percy back to Boston after Lexington.

" 'Twas Warren who made the army, children," Father told us. "Warren who wrote the circular that went out all over, telling of Lexington and Concord, and brought the men in from as far as a hundred miles hence, to Harvard Yard. Here, let me read it to you, so you know what he has done."

No more Doctor Warren, our family friend. He's general of the Massachusetts troops now. My father holds him up to us as a hero.

The hero was here last night. Drinking with my father. Warren is not a drinking man. He is an honored physician. But last night he acted the fool.

Dulce et decorum est pro patria mori, I heard him say.

I asked my father, afterward, what that meant.

He said it means "I hope I shall die up to my knees in blood."

Madness. They're all as mad as hooty owls. Foolishness to throw up those earthworks on that hill at Charlestown. Even Father said the British will move across the river and destroy them. Well, it's a fine time for him to decide that now, isn't it?

Last night Warren said he was going to fight.

"Going to the hill," he told Rachel, like he

was talking about going to a frolic. I stood listening in the shadows of the hall.

"Don't be a fool," Rachel told him. And again there was that familiarity in their conversation. As a woman has when she is comfortable with a man and must no longer use flattery to please him. It was her way with him. She ofttimes teased him.

My sister Debby says they have settled into this way so they can cover their fondness for one another.

I do not know what to think. Debby says I do not believe it because I am too smitten with Warren myself. And I am jealous.

Debby is right.

But she hates him. And she tricked me into hating him, too. And into saying words to him that shame me. And now this thing lies between me and Warren, sick and in need of fixing. And Warren is no longer a doctor, but a general, talking about going to the hill today and dying up to his knees in blood.

"For all you've done raising an army, you couldn't command a group of bell ringers at the Cockerel," Rachel told him last night.

"Just the same, dear girl, I'm going. Come have a glass of wine with me."

"Don't be silly, Joseph." And Rachel had come out of the parlor, tears streaming down her face. She had run out of teasing things to say. Her way didn't work anymore. "Has the whole world gone mad?" she said to me in passing. "He's so young and alive. Why does he want a rendezvous with death?" And without waiting for an answer, she'd run upstairs. Later I heard her sobbing in her room.

So there it was, plain as the nose on your face. And I thought, Debby is right. There is something more than friendship between them. Debby had thought so all along. Only Father didn't see it.

What matters, Father? What's true? Or what people think?

Warren left late. He and my father were both in their cups. I think Father did it on purpose. "He'll not go to the hill today," he told Rachel at breakfast. "He'll stay in bed, nursing his head."

"DON'T LET ANYONE disturb your father today," Rachel instructed me this morning. "He's printing money." Then she went to attend baby

Joshua, who is teething and fretful. She took him out for some air. An hour ago she brought him home sleeping. And went upstairs herself, for a nap. And the house got quiet until the minister came up the walk.

"Is your father to home? I'm Reverend William Gordon from Roxbury. I would speak with him."

"About what?"

"I've been traveling the countryside this past month, talking to those who were at Lexington and Concord. I would ask him about his ride."

Another one, I minded. They come almost every day. How do they find us?

"What ride?" I asked, pretending ignorance. I have found lately that it is a great boon to be simpleminded. "He took many rides."

"Is he here?" he asked again.

"He's working in his shop."

"Would you ask, please, if he would see me?"

So I asked. My father looked up from his work. "Tell him to come back later," he said. "I'm busy now. Tell him to come back in an hour."

"Why don't you just say no?" I asked.

Foolish question. Could he ever say no? To

Grandmother, when she terrorized us? To his customers, who owed him so much money? To the Sons of Liberty or the Committee of Safety, when they asked him to take all those rides?

" 'Twouldn't be seemly, him a man of God. He's educated. Likely at Harvard." Having gone no further than North Writing School, my father has great respect for education.

"Tell him 'later' and mayhap he won't come back," he advised.

But now the man *was* back, coming through the gate, down the walk. I opened the door. Cannon pounded. He waited until the sound was finished, then he spoke.

"Can your father see me now?"

He was drenched with sweat. "Wait," I said. Then I ran through the house and down the two steps in back to the shop.

"What's acting?" Father asked. "Is it Warren? Has he stopped by yet this day?"

"No. The minister is back."

"I said later."

"It is later."

My eyes met those of John Cook, who'd just come in the back door. His father owned the house. My breath caught. In the month we'd been here, he and I had become friends. Being friends with a boy was new to me. Though my sister Debby did it all the time. John was apprenticing with my father.

"Is the sentry coming?" my father asked John.

"Yessir. He thought he'd be needed on the hill. Was ready to go fight. But they told him he was more needed here."

A guard was posted outside the shop all the time. My father's press must not be left without protection. Money was needed desperately by the province of Massachusetts.

They needed it to make war. So every day my father and John worked, betimes twelve hours, making six-shilling and four-pound notes. Billy Dawes, who'd ridden with Father the night before Lexington, had smuggled Father's small press, copper plates, and tools out of Boston. Copper and paper were hard to come by.

"These notes are worthless," Father said to John. "I'm ashamed of them. So thick. The British laugh at us. Call them pasteboard currency."

"Pasteboard currency is a sight better than none," John said.

"Father, what shall I tell the minister?"

He got off his stool. He wiped his hands with

a rag and looked at me. "You must speak to him, Sarah. I can't."

"Me?" I was dumbfounded. And angry. He wasn't going to put this off on me. I wouldn't let him. "You mean you won't."

"All right, I won't."

"Why?"

"Many reasons, Sarah. Reason one, as John Adams would say, because I can scarce think for worrying that my friend Doctor Warren will take it in his head to go to the hill today. Has he been around?"

"No."

"Good. Likely he's still sleeping it off. He won't go unless he stops here first. He promised me."

I tried not to show any feeling in my face. "And? Reason two?"

"Because I already gave a deposition about Lexington. To the Provincial Congress."

"They gave it back to you."

"Yes." He threw the rag down, reached for a pitcher of cider, and poured himself a cup. "It was displeasing to them. Not one they wanted to send to England with hundreds of others on Derby's schooner."

"Why?" I asked.

"Because I told how I almost attacked a British patrol. The Whigs don't want anyone in London to think of us as aggressors. They want us to be regarded as innocent."

Innocent. My father belabored the word.

He gulped his cider. "My God, we're anything but innocent, Sarah. We started this thing as well as they did. But Warren, who is in charge of propaganda, doesn't want that out. I've still to settle that with him."

So we both have things to settle with him then, I thought. I watched Father as he stared into the cup, brooding. He was a handsome man in his own way. Not a fine figure of a man like Doctor Warren. Father was short. And somewhat rotund. But he was a good man, a decent man, and kindly.

He was a good father. I loved him. But in this last year he had turned our lives around. A war had started. Men in Massachusetts had started it. All on their own.

My father had been one of them. I know betimes the thought afflicted him. He wasn't like Sam Adams, pushing for war.

And we didn't even know if the rest of the

colonies would back us in this war. Might be, they wouldn't. That they'd let us stand against England all on our own.

Nobody knew the rules for doing that, for breaking with the mother country or making war. We were on new ground now, making up the rules each morning when we got out of bed. Men like John and Sam Adams and John Hancock were this minute riding to the congress in Philadelphia to find out what the rules would be.

"Go and talk to the man, Sarah," Father said softly. "You have my permission to tell him anything he wants to know about us."

"I don't know what to say to him."

"Yes, you do. You're a young lady now. Thirteen last January."

"Why is it that I'm a young lady for something like this and still a little girl whenever Grandmother scolds?"

He smiled. "My little lamb," he said, "a young woman already. And lovely. Isn't she, John?"

"Father!" I chided him and blushed. I saw John blush, too.

"You know I love you, Sarah," Father said. "You've always been my favorite."

"After Debby."

"You'll do it then?"

"What do I *say* to the man, Father? What does he want of us?"

He hesitated for a moment, then spoke plain. "He's going to ask you if I know who fired the first shot, Sarah. That's what he wants from us."

Oh, that. The first shot at Lexington. I'd come upon him and Rachel discussing it in low tones, once or twice of late.

"He will think that is why the Whigs returned my deposition to me. You must tell him why it was returned. Tell him about my attacking the British patrol. Do you understand?"

"Yes," I said, though I did not. I had too many questions to ask. But this was not the time.

In the last few years, since he'd started working for the Sons and all those committees, my father had turned into a keeper of secrets. We became accustomed to it in our family.

If we hadn't, we wouldn't still be a family.

But since the eighteenth of April, when he'd sneaked out of Boston to take his small boat across the Charles, where they had a horse waiting for him, my father had been locked inside himself. Further than he'd been after my mother had died. But in a different way, now.

Then, he was hurting for himself. Now, he was hurting for others. And behaving as if he alone were accountable for what all those meetings and rides had wrought.

"You will do it then?" he asked.

"Yes, Father."

His smile was sad. "You're my fine girl, Sarah."

I nodded.

"Remember what we always talk about? What you always ask me? 'Father,' you say, 'what matters? What's true? Or what people think?' And what do I always say, Sarah?"

"What's true," I answered. I wanted to ask, *But what* is *true? Who* did *fire the first shot? Do you know? And will you keep it a secret forever?*

But I didn't push the matter. John was paying mind, sensing something. I couldn't allow that. John's eyes were blue and very becalmed. He was completely besotted with my father. The famous Paul Revere; the British spy, Private Howe had called him.

"All right, Father," I said, "I'll do it." And I started out of the shop.

"Sarah?"

"Yes, Father?"

"Tell me soon as Warren stops around."

"Yes, Father."

Chapter Two

I INVITED HIM IN and sat him down. I gave him cider.

"How can I help you, Reverend?"

Out of his haversack he took ink, a quill pen, and paper—all of which he spread on a table. "Do you know aught about your father's ride?" he asked again.

"Which ride? He took many."

"Don't play with me, child. The ride that is on everyone's tongue these days."

"Isn't that the way of it, though? My father made at least five journeys to New York and Philadelphia in the last two years, Reverend. No one came around asking about them."

"None were like the ride to Lexington."

"They led up to it."

"Be that as it may. Your father is famous now. Everyone wants to know about him."

Famous, is he? If he could see my father in that back room, the heat and flies coming in the window, copper plates all about, the smell of ink so pungent, the floor full of grimy sand and bits of paper, him wiping the sweat from his eyes as he lowers the platen on the press, tightens the screws, and swears because the paper for the last batch of money cost six dollars a ream when it was worth only four.

My father does not consider himself famous. Miserable, yes, but not famous.

"Tell me how he rode out of Boston that night to Lexington."

"There was no more riding out of Boston by that time. He was a wanted man. He had to sneak out and take a small boat across the Charles."

"Ah, yes." He wrote feverishly, as if my words were jewels to be cherished.

I became angry. What right did he have to

walk in here and think he could hear all this just for the asking? So he could write it down and make sense of it when none of us in this house yet could?

"Tell me what it is like to be the daughter of Paul Revere," he said.

Dear God, was he daft? "Do you hear the guns, Reverend?"

"Yes."

"People are dying. Good people. And my father helped start the fighting."

He stopped writing. He looked at me as if I had uncommon powers.

"He and his friends started this war. And we don't know yet if the other colonies are in this fight with us. Or if we are in it alone. But there is no turning back."

He stared at me with watery blue fish eyes. "You must not take this upon yourself, child. What is happening today has been coming on for years."

"My father has been part of it for years. It is not something he takes lightly."

He sighed and nodded. "Tell me your recollections."

"My recollections are my own."

"No, child. They belong to the world now. You owe the telling."

Indeed! And was I to be left with nothing, then? What of my feelings? Very well, I decided, I would tell him things. But I would confuse him.

And so I started telling.

"I was a child when my father started his political nonsense. That's what my own dead mama called it. I recollect him coming in with soot all over his face after a night out with the Sons. It was part of our lives. I can tell you that."

He commenced writing again.

"I can tell you how my stepmother, Rachel, came to us. And how we needed her to be a family again after my mother died. And how my father's work for the Sons of Liberty and the Provincial Congress near ruined all that."

"Yes, talk to me of this, child."

God help me. I told the man everything but what he wanted to know.

I told him about Grandmother and her vile moods. And how my sister the first Mary was born under the smallpox flag and died a year later. And how my sister Isanna died. And Mother was buried under a tombstone with a skull and crossbones on it.

He wrote it down, all of it.

I told him how the British made a ditty about my father and Doctor Warren after they threw the tea off the ships. And how my father made teeth for Doctor Warren this spring. "Two, made out of one piece of ivory. And held in place with wire. One was an eyetooth."

He wrote furiously.

I told him how my brother Paul left North Writing School and went to work in Father's shop. And how he was left behind in Boston to keep the house and shop in order. "Paul's fifteen. And he's there all alone. He had to turn two muskets over to the king's men," I said.

The reverend was beginning to look confused. *Good,* I thought. *It serves you right for thinking I will tell you what you want to know just for the asking.*

"Ruffles, our dog, followed my father to the boat that last night in Boston, when he made his ride. Paul and I had to go and get Ruffles."

He put it down.

"My father tied rags around the oars of the boat that took him across the Charles that night. To muffle the sound. And they rowed right under the HMS *Somerset* in the harbor. She's got sixty-four guns and is a great ship of the line."

He wrote that, too.

"Before he left Boston, my father helped his friend Isaiah Thomas smuggle his printing press out."

That pleased him. He smiled.

"My sister Debby is the beautiful one. But she has marks on her face from the pox. I don't. But I'm not beautiful, either. My grandmother favors Debby. I think Grandmother hates me a little because I didn't get pox marks. Debby is her favorite, being named after her, you see."

He scribbled.

"My mama died hard. 'What will happen to my children?' she asked everyone. I was there when she asked it. The wives of my father's friends in the Masons and the North Caucus and the Sons would never have anything to do with her. They thought themselves of a higher order, those wives."

He nodded, but this he did not mark down. This was not what he wanted from me.

I pondered if I should tell him about Billy Dawes, who rode with my father that night. And how Billy sneaked back into Boston afterward. Every Saturday, for weeks. And his sister in

Boston covered gold pieces with cloth and sewed them on his coat as buttons. So he could smuggle money out.

No, I decided. I must protect Billy Dawes.

"What else would you have me tell you, Reverend?"

The poor man looked addled. He commenced to speak, then the cannon started up again and he fell silent, though his lips moved as if in prayer. I minded that he was praying for those poor souls on the hill.

When the cannon stopped, he smiled. "Child, all you have said is interesting. But I would ask you one question."

I nodded.

"Did your father ever say who fired the first shot at Lexington?"

"The first shot?"

"Yes. He was there."

"He was running across Lexington Common with John Hancock's trunk of important papers. Mr. Lowell was helping him. They were taking it into the woods."

"I heard that story. Some say he turned and saw who fired the first shot."

"I don't know, Reverend. I never heard tell."

"Did he say why his deposition was returned to him by Whig leaders?"

"Because he wrote in it how he near attacked a British patrol. They did not want such information to go to England. They do not want England to think we started this thing."

"Some people think your father knows who fired the first shot," he persisted.

"It's not what people think that matters, Reverend. It's what's true."

He saw I was not about to be pushed. "Do you have anything else to tell me?"

I thought for a moment. "Yes. And it's very sad."

He waited.

"The horse my father rode that night was named Brown Beauty. She belonged to a man named Larkin in Charlestown. She was a fine horse, sure of foot and swift, great of heart. The British took her from Father that night. A British grenadier rode her. He was a heavy man, and she was already spent. My father thinks this British man rode her to death. Killed her."

"I'm sorry," he said. Then he gathered together his things. "Have you ever asked your father, outright, if he saw who fired the first shot?"

"No, sir."

"You might want to do that sometime, Sarah Revere." Then he got to his feet. "Oh, by the way, tell your father that General Gage has booked passage on the *Charming Nancy* for his wife. He is sending her to England."

That brought me up short. *Margaret? To England?* "But she's American," I said. "Why would he do that?"

"Because someone told Doctor Warren about Gage's plan to march on Concord last April for the military stores. There are those who think that someone was Gage's own wife."

Margaret Gage. Fancy that. And then I stood stock-still, taken by a thought. It was something Rachel had said when we were coming out of Boston last month. We were stopped at the British sentry post and there we met her friend Lady Frankland coming back in.

What have we wrought, Lady Frankland? asked Rachel.

We are, in part, responsible you and I, Rachel. Are you sorry?

No, Rachel had answered. We did what was right to do. But I fear for Margaret.

I couldn't think. Too many thoughts were

crowding my mind. I must go somewhere and be alone and ponder it.

"Did you know Mrs. Gage?" he was asking.

"No, sir. I only knew of her."

He nodded slowly, thanked me, and I saw him out the door.

I stood watching him walk down the path. Then I poured myself a glass of cold cider, picked up a shirt I was working on for my father, and went out back through the kitchen garden.

There was an arbor at the end, with a bench. I ofttimes went there of an afternoon to do my sewing when the house became too crowded for me. We lived with so many people now. Henry Knox and his wife, Lucy, and the Cooks. It's a large house, but just as crowded as we were at home in Boston.

I sat down in the coolness. Rachel will wake soon, I told myself. And then I will tell her what I heard about Margaret Gage.

Rachel will want to know. I must tell her.

Oh God, Rachel! I can scarce form the question in my mind. Was it Margaret Gage, then, who informed Doctor Warren? And is this what Rachel and Lady Frankland felt so responsible for? That if she hadn't informed him, there would have been no fight at Lexington? And now no war?

Rachel! Think of it! So close to Doctor Warren. Was this the reason? Or was it because what was between Rachel and Warren was more than friendship? How am I to know?

Is anything to be made clear to me? There are too many secrets in this family.

I recollect the night Rachel asked Doctor Warren if he would see Mrs. Gage as a patient. And the look that passed between them.

Did Rachel send Mrs. Gage to him to be an informer?

I will have no peace until I find out these things.

And what about me? Will I be able to set right, this day, this terrible thing that lies between me and Doctor Warren? Before he goes to the hill? He'll go, I know he will.

I must put it all together in my head and make sense of it. Before he gets here. Before Rachel wakes up.

I'll do it now. I'll sit and study on it. From here I can see the front walk, can see if Doctor Warren comes by. The windows are all open. I'll hear Rachel come downstairs.

I'll sit here and think on things so I know what to say to them, all of them.

Oh, I wish those guns weren't so loud. I wish I didn't feel that time was growing so short.

Father, what matters? What people think? Or what's true?

I'll figure it out.

Boston

Chapter Three

*I*F WHAT people think matters, then my father met Rachel in the street outside his shop and brought her home.

And when George Robert Twelvetrees Hewes stole a piece of roast veal from the larder when he was inoculated for the pox back in 1764, he should have died from the eating. For to eat meat after inoculation is to invite death.

And Phyllis, slave wife of slave Mark, was strangled before she was burned at the stake years ago for her part in poisoning her master.

These are the tales they tell in Boston. The

things they think are true. The tales Grandmother keeps alive.

What *is* true is that Phyllis was not strangled first. She was burned alive. George Robert Twelvetrees Hewes recovered from inoculation faster than the others for eating meat.

And my father never laid eyes on Rachel Walker until Paul and I brought her home.

Our mother died in May of '73, five months after birthing Isanna. God brooded on our house. Isanna was always sickly. My father went about his business as if someone had put a curse on him, saying "bad cess to Paul Revere."

He curled up inside himself. Evenings when he wasn't at North End Caucus or the Masons, he was with Doctor Warren, who was himself a widower with four young children in the care of their grandmother in the country. Warren oft-times came to our house on the way home from a sick call at night. The two men were as unlike as night and day. But they belonged to the same political clubs and were friends since the Stamp Act days. They'd worked together in Benjamin Edes's *Gazette* office at the time of the Boston Massacre. All the leading Whigs in Boston were married. Both widowers now, Father and Doctor

Warren shared many a mug of flip at the Salutation after meetings were over.

We children were left to Grandmother's iron rule. She made us work hard sweeping, polishing, carrying, scrubbing. She even blamed us for Mama's death, saying if we'd tended to our chores, Mama would not have died.

We could not abide Father anymore as he was. We could abide Grandmother less. If we had to grow up under her, we would all perish. She was as mean as a hornet. And there was no accounting for it. She had the best room in the house, her own cordwood, her cooking rights, and pots on the hearth that no one touched. Her own gooseberry bushes in the yard that we dared not dry our clothes on.

I was eleven that year, Paul thirteen, Mary nine, Frances seven, Elizabeth three, and Debby fifteen and already running with Amos Lincoln— when his master, the carpenter Thomas Crafts, let him run.

Grandmother could not keep a rein on Debby, did not even wish to. If we didn't find a mother soon, Debby would have to marry Amos and likely be brought to bed of a child eight months after. As Mama had done with Debby herself.

And while that was no great scandal in our time, Debby was not Mama. She was young and silly and didn't know what she was about.

I'd seen Debby and Amos beside Father's new barn one night that summer of '73. Debby was leaning against it. Amos was kissing her.

He had his hand under her dress.

"I'm going to tell Father!" I'd yelled at her after an abashed Amos had left.

She laughed. "You do and I'll tell Grandmother that you were talking to Agnes Surriage in the market last week. Bringing yourself down to the level of a lowly scullery maid."

"She's Lady Frankland now. She's *been* that for years. And she's a neighbor."

"She'll always be a scullery maid."

"If anyone is bringing herself down to such a level, it's you, Debby. What would Mama say?"

She gave me a hard look. "Mama's gone." But there were tears in her eyes. "And all *he* cares about is the silver coffeepot he's making for Paul Dudley Sargent."

She meant Father. "He cares about us. He's just brooding."

I hated Debby and loved her all at the same time. Many a day I ended up doing her chores while she ran the streets, so little Frances or Mary wouldn't have to do them.

Part of why Grandmother spoiled her so was because she flattered, cajoled, contrived, and lied to get her own way. It was not her fault. She had learned it was the way to survive with the old lady after Mama died.

Things were not good in our house. I knew I must do something to bring Father out of his shell. But what?

The night after I'd argued with Debby, Paul and I were playing on the streets, out after curfew. We were spying on Reverend Barnard.

Barnard was over eighty. He owned the house next to ours. All year he lived in Marblehead, but on his birthday he came to sleep in the house where he'd first drawn breath.

His birthday was the twenty-seventh of August. People said he had uncommon powers and he came home to invoke the spirits of the dead in that empty house. All the children in the neighborhood spied on him. But none were allowed to stay up late enough to find out why he burned candles all night.

It was a hot night, smelling of sweet woodsmoke and the sea. The little ones were abed.

Debby was out with Amos. Paul and I had sneaked out, determined to stay as far into the night as it took to see what old Barnard was about.

Paul was standing on some barrels, peeking in Barnard's side window.

"What do you see?" I asked. I stood watch in the alley.

"He's mumbling over a book. And cooking something on the hearth. I think it's eye of newt."

Paul had a quick mind. He was always fancying tales. He took after our French Huguenot father.

"Likely it's barley water." I had the Yankee mind, like Mama.

"Wait a minute, he's not mumbling. He's talking to someone."

"Who?"

"I don't know. There's no one in the room with him that I can see. But he's having a lively discussion."

I felt a chill.

"Ho there, you children, what are you doing there spying on that old man? And why are you out after curfew?"

It was Mr. Shaw, the tailor, in his blue coat and best wig, sporting his gold cane. "You're Paul Revere's brats, aren't you? Well, we'll see what your father has to say about this. Get down from that barrel there, you!"

Paul scrambled down.

"Now come along." Shaw grabbed Paul roughly by the arm. "I'll see you to your front door."

"My father is out," I said quickly.

"Well, your grandmother will do. She still knows how to wield a switch, I hear."

"Are those Paul Revere's children? They're waiting for me."

The sweet voice came through the dark like an angel would sound. If I believed in angels. Which I didn't, because people who did had popes in their bellies. Which is what they said in Boston about anyone who was sympathetic to Catholics or their ways.

"Miss Walker." Mr. Shaw dropped Paul's arm to take off his hat to her. "Are you telling me these rude children are waiting for you?"

"Of course. They were to meet me and escort me to their father's shop. I've need to see his wares, and he couldn't be here this evening. Hello, Paul. Hello, Sarah."

We stared. We'd seen her about on North Square, same as we'd seen a lot of people. But we'd never met her.

"How is baby Isanna?" she asked.

"Doing poorly." Paul, with his quickness, minded that she was offering to help. "Is it the silver-backed looking glass you're after?"

"Yes. Will you show it to me?"

Paul bowed. "I'd be honored."

Then he looked at me. "This is the lady Agnes Surriage told us of when we met her in the market last week, Sarah. Don't you remember?"

"Of course." But I'd quite forgotten. Agnes Surriage, or Lady Frankland, had dropped a package. Her little nigra boy had his arms full. Paul picked it up for her. Awash in silk and lace, she'd smiled and spoken with us.

"And how is your dear father these days? When I married my Harry, your parents were of the few in this town who would speak to me."

Before we'd known what we were about, we'd told her of our father's melancholy. "He needs a new lady friend," she'd said. "I'll send that nice Rachel Walker by."

Agnes was a Tory. Her husband, Sir Harry, dead now, had once been Collector of the Port.

But Father said he had never bothered merchants when they went against the navigation acts of England and smuggled.

"I told you Miss Walker would be around soon, didn't I, Sarah?" Paul asked. "Are you coming?"

I smiled at Mr. Shaw and ran after them, right to our front door, while that esteemed gentleman stood with his mouth open, not knowing whether to apologize or shake his gold cane at us.

That is how we brought our new stepmother home for the first time. It is true. Not what people think. And it matters.

Just before we went in the front door, a thought came to me and I tugged at Rachel's arm.

"Yes, Sarah?"

"I think you oughtn't to tell our grandmother that Lady Frankland sent you. She hates Lady Frankland."

She smiled. "Lady Frankland didn't send me, Sarah. No one sends me anywhere. She simply reminded me what lovely silver hand mirrors your father makes. He is the finest silversmith around, you know. Now stop worrying so."

She met my eyes with her own. And from that moment we were friends.

Baby Isanna was screaming when we went inside. Grandmother, who could usually quiet her, was having no luck.

"Get me a sugar teat!" she ordered as we came in the door. "Where have you two been? Sneaked out the window again, I suppose! If I wasn't so tired, I'd switch you both."

She would, too.

Then she saw Rachel. "Who is this?"

"Grandmother, this is Rachel Walker," Paul said. "She wants to see Father."

The old lady took her measure. "I'll wager she does. Half the women in Boston do. You're a plainer piece than some of the others who've come round asking to see his wares."

"Grandmother!" I was at the kitchen hearth, dipping a cloth in sugar water and winding it tight for Isanna to suck on. While it was true that Rachel wasn't pretty, she wasn't an offense to the eye, either.

"It's all right, Sarah, I don't mind," she said.

"Mind? I'll say who's to mind what in this house. Without me, they'd all be living in filth. Well? What do you want with my son?"

"I heard he makes the loveliest silver hand mirrors." Rachel stepped forward and held out her arms for the baby.

Grandmother handed Isanna over. And as soon as Rachel took the child, Isanna stopped crying. This was no mean feat, and even Grandmother was taken with it.

"Sit," she invited. "Sarah, make tea. You know where I keep my supply."

I hesitated. Grandmother drank her tea. The rest of us didn't. The small tax on it was the only remnant of the trouble with the Crown we had now. But trouble it still was, and my father said there would soon be more. He forbade tea in the house. This, though the Patriots were all fighting amongst themselves, and people in Boston were tired of mob activities and the dire predictions of Sam Adams.

"Well?" Grandmother snapped. "What are you waiting for, Sarah?"

"Mayhap Rachel doesn't drink tea," I said.

"Nonsense. Everyone drinks tea these days. Everyone's importing it. Even John Adams."

"He's gone back to Braintree," Paul put in.

"What?" Grandmother asked. "Who cares where he goes? Good riddance to him, I say.

43

Him and the Hancocks. Everyone knows they made their money through smuggling. And oh, I could tell you things about young John Hancock's aunt Lydia. Now do you take tea or not, Rachel Walker?"

I saw the trap. So did Paul. If Father came in and found Rachel drinking tea, he would take an immediate dislike to her. But she'd offend Grandmother if she didn't accept it.

"Of course I'll have tea," Rachel said brightly. "I love a good cup as well as anyone."

Either the woman had decided it was better to cosy up to Grandmother or she was completely ignorant of my father's activities. She started to sit down.

"Not there!" Grandmother snapped. "That's my chair."

Rachel stared at her for a moment, then spoke softly. "It's by the window. I thought the cool fresh air would soothe Isanna."

They faced each other. Paul and I waited, each holding our breath, knowing the balance of our future lay in Rachel's ability to stand up to Grandmother.

The old woman was tired. It showed in her voice when she spoke. "Certain things in this house are mine. I pay board. I have my chair, my sewing corner, my room, my pots, my food in the larder. If I so much as borrow a bit of sugar, I put it back."

"As it should be," Rachel said, still poised beside the chair.

"Your mother was Rachel Carlile, was she not?" Grandmother asked.

"Yes."

"I knew two of your great-aunts. They lived in the Foster house, close to the one we once rented from Doctor Clark."

"Yes," Rachel said again. "And your people helped found the colonies. Your great-grand-father was fined in court for speaking against the government."

"That would be Thomas Dexter, yes. Back in 1632. The Hitchbourns have always been thorns in the side of government." Grandmother was proud of that, but not proud enough to give up her tea.

"You've been given a good education, I hear. How old are you?" she asked Rachel.

"Old enough to know how to care for a babe such as this," Rachel said, "and to see that you need a spell of rest."

"Hmmph," Grandmother said. "Are you getting that tea, Sarah?"

"Yes, Grandmother."

"Well, the baby seems in good hands. I'm going to bed. You may sit in my chair, Rachel Walker. For tonight."

Rachel sat. And she was still sitting there holding a sleeping Isanna, sipping her second cup of tea, when Father came in half an hour later.

He took no note of the brew she was drinking. His eyes went soft when he saw her holding his baby. He patted Paul's head, then mine, called us his lambs, and sent us to bed.

I believe that when Isanna died in the middle of September, Father would have gone completely into the grip of melancholy, if not for Rachel.

He married her on the tenth day of October. But first he courted her, properlike. He even wrote her poetry. I found one of those poems written on the back of a bill in his shop.

I loved Rachel because she made Father come alive again. She pulled him free of the grip of darkness that surrounded him.

And because she was the first person Grandmother couldn't ride roughshod over.

Rachel gave the old woman her place in the house but wouldn't be bullied. She never sat in Grandmother's chair again. Peace came to our house.

"As it should be," Rachel told us.

But peace didn't last. And I didn't trust it.

Chapter Four

*W*E HAD PEACE for one month after they married. In that month, my father hired a chaise and took Rachel on a wedding trip to the Blue Hills of Milton, where they spent time with friends. He took her rowing on the Charles twice, while we children watched from the shore with our blanket spread beneath us and a basket of food ready for their return.

Rachel proved to be a good stepmother. She was young and strong and went about the chores with a cheerful determination, dividing them up equally between us, making sure we had time to play.

She knew how to use herbs in her cooking. She made a wonderful dish of quinces in sugar. First she boiled them in water over the fire, then took them out and pared them, took their weight in loaf sugar, and put it all into a kettle with more water until a syrup formed.

She'd send us to market for oranges, and put them in, too. Since my father was clerk of the North End Market that year—and his job was to keep peace among the bargainers and to see that no one was cheated—we got the best oranges.

The only problem Rachel had was shooing us children out of the kitchen so we weren't underfoot.

"Take the little ones out to play!" she'd say to me. "They need the sun. Winter will soon be upon us."

"You'll spoil them!" Grandmother would yell at her. "You're bedeviling all that I've trained them up to be."

She ignored Grandmother and won all our hearts. No longer did Paul have to stand over a bubbling cauldron doing dishes when he made the mistake of treading barn dirt in on the clean floorboards.

She made him sweep out the dirt and that was

the end of it. Paul was shy of her. But he kept the cordwood coming for her fire and fetched and carried for her without being asked.

She could knead bread dough, make the fixings for soup, and pin up Debby's hair before she went out, all at the same time, it seemed.

One night, just after they returned from their wedding trip, Rachel was preparing a meat pie for supper and fixing Debby's hair. "And who is this Amos Lincoln?" she teased. "Why don't you bring him round?"

Debby was sitting on a chair by the hearth, smiling like a pleased cat. She was going to a frolic with Amos. "Nobody's asked me to."

"Well, I am. I make a proper clam pie, you know. Does he like clam pie?"

"Yes."

"I could teach you if you wanted to learn. Didn't your father tell you that's why he married me? For my clam pie?"

"Bah!" Grandmother got out of her chair and started for the stairs. "I've a headache from all this worthless prattle. The air is getting thick in here. I'll take my supper in my room."

Debby flushed. "Don't mind Grandmother, Rachel."

"I don't."

"She gets jealous if I pay you mind."

"Then you must be extra nice to her."

Debby stood up and of a sudden kissed her. "Thank you, Rachel, mayhap I will bring Amos by. Later tonight?"

"We'll keep a candle in the window."

"Rachel? I must needs talk," I said when Debby left.

"Do." She was rolling dough for tomorrow's bread. "But set those dishes on the table at the same time."

I did so. "Rachel, you should know. Elizabeth sometimes has nightmares. And when she does, she wets her bed."

"Yes, I know. It would be good if she could be broken of the habit before winter comes."

"She's only three. She started wetting when Mama died. And Isanna dying so soon after didn't help. I know how to stop Elizabeth, but Grandmother won't let me try."

"How?"

"If she could have Ruffles in the room with her."

Rachel looked up from her kneading. "The dog?"

"Yes. Mama always allowed it. Grandmother won't. I know Elizabeth misses him. Grandmother makes him stay in the barn at night. And he cries. And winter is coming."

She smiled. "Bring him in tonight."

"Are you sure it will be all right?"

"Yes. Is that all? I thought the problem was serious."

"No, there's more. Rachel, Mary thinks she is going to die."

"I heard her asking your father the other day to make sure they didn't bury her under the ground."

I nodded. "She has a dreaded fear of it. Because of Mama, too," I explained. "But it's also got to do with the first Mary."

"The first?"

"Yes. In '64 the smallpox epidemic came. Debby got it. The selectmen wanted Father to put her in the pesthouse. He wouldn't. So we were all confined. And the flag was hung in front of the house. A baby was born under it and died in a year. They had called her Mary. Grandmother is always telling us the story about it. Little Mary thinks she should die, too. Because of her name."

"So what must we do about that?"

"I think we should take her to Old Granary."

"The graveyard?"

"Yes. I think if she saw the first Mary's grave, it would mark the difference between them. She's never been allowed to go there."

"Then we shall take her."

"It's where Mama's buried," I said.

"All the more reason we should go."

I set another dish down on the table and hesitated. "There's more, Rachel."

"I supposed there would be. Go on."

"Frances wants to be a boy. Grandmother whips her for dressing up in my brother's old clothing. But she does it just the same."

"Am I to know why?"

"She said she doesn't want to grow up and be a woman and be brought to bed of a child and die."

"I see." A lock of dark hair had escaped her mobcap. She brushed it aside. "Have you any remedy for that?"

"No, I thought you would."

"Well, and your grandmother told me this family was wondrous dull."

"We're not that."

"Let me study on the Frances problem for a while. What of you, Sarah? Have you any quiverings or quakes?"

I blushed. "I'm just glad you've come to us," I said.

She went back to her work, pondering. "When?" she asked, "was the last time Frances had a new dress and bonnet?"

"Last year. She wears my old ones. Though she has one good one for church."

"She's seven. Old enough for her first English gown, wouldn't you say?"

"Oh, Rachel! What a wonderful thought!" I beamed.

"I liked playing at being a boy, too," she said. "Until my mother made my first English gown. Fabric from France, it was. I'll never forget it."

That night Rachel let Ruffles in the house.

"Bah," Grandmother said as I fetched her meat pie to her room. It was a commodious room, only a bit smaller than that of my parents.

"Grandmother told me your family was wondrous dull," Grandmother mimicked. "If it's dullness she's after, she's due for a fall. I take it she knows naught of your father's activities."

I set the tray down on a small table. "If she

doesn't, she'll not hear it from me, Grandmother. And you shouldn't have been eavesdropping."

She took the dish of meat pie, tasted it, and smacked her lips. "She's a fair hand at cooking, I'll give her that. But we'll see how she acts when she finds out about your father."

There was a reason Grandmother wore black all the time. It was in keeping with her disposition. She saw the dark in everything, not the light. She sought out the dark in people. When someone was having trouble, she was the first to know and speak of it.

If someone had good fortune, she had little use for them. She was drawn to hard luck. She relished it. All her stories of the past were calculated to scare the hose off us. Her dire predictions for us all, with the exception of Debby, were frequent and uttered with certainty.

"I'm sure Father has told Rachel everything there is to tell, Grandmother."

"He's a fool if he did. She never would have wed him. What woman would?"

"Well, it matters little now, anyway. All his activities have come to a halt."

She eyed me through narrow spectacles. "You haven't heard, then, about the arrival of the tea?"

"What tea?"

She chuckled. "The East India Company has forty million weight of tea rotting in its warehouses along the Thames. And the company is near bankrupt. The British government has decided to ship the tea here to save the company. Give it the American market."

Gravy dribbled on her bewhiskered chin. She wiped it away. Grandmother was of a political turn of mind. Bright as a newly minted shilling, she could discuss every political vagary of the day.

"You didn't hear your precious Doctor Warren speaking about it with your father the other night when he was here?"

I blushed. Of late I'd been clumsy and awkward in Doctor Warren's presence. I did not know why. And I hadn't thought that anyone had paid mind. Apparently Grandmother had.

Her eyes gleamed wickedly. "The tea ships are expected in November. Already your father and his friends are in full stride, plotting. Wait. Ha! Wait until darling Rachel finds out what she's gotten herself into!"

I thought it mean of her to say such. Rachel was a shaft of sunlight in the house, after months of hearing my grandmother reciting how God had punished us all for our misbehavior by taking our mother.

Besides which, I was confident that Rachel knew what she had gotten herself into. She wasn't a dull woman.

I was wrong. Rachel wasn't dull, but she could fit in her thimble what she knew about my father's activities.

By the first week in November, word was all over town about the tea ships. Broadsides announced meetings. The Sons of Liberty, who seemed to have disappeared that summer, were in full stride again. In the street one heard the names Will Molineaux, John Rowe, and John Hancock on everyone's lips.

My father and Doctor Warren's friends were back in town. We children knew what to expect.

Father went about his business in his shop quietly. But we didn't lack our share of mysterious knockings on our door in the middle of the night and whispered voices below stairs. Looking out the upstairs window, I'd see a lantern in the barn and know Paul was saddling up Militia, my father's new mare. It was all familiar. We children were accustomed to it.

Rachel wasn't. At breakfast her face was often

drawn. Many times Father's place was empty at the table. He'd come in before we were through eating, bleary-eyed and happy, peck Rachel on the cheek, nod to his mother, chuck Elizabeth under the chin, say something funny to Mary and Frances, give Debby some bit of gossip from the street, ask Paul about his lessons, pat me and Ruffles on the head, then enjoy a big breakfast of ham, fish, biscuits, and eggs.

Times like this, I watched Rachel's face. It was a mask. I saw nothing amiss. But the twinkle in Grandmother's eyes grew brighter.

My mother had trained us not to ask Father about his activities. By the second week in November we didn't have to. We got word on the street.

The *Dartmouth,* first of the tea ships, was to arrive soon. "The Body," which was what my father and his cohorts were called, had met at Faneuil Hall, then ordered Mr. Rotch, owner of the *Dartmouth,* to tie her up at Griffin's Wharf.

My father was one of twenty-five men selected to watch her once she docked, so the tea wouldn't be unloaded.

It was the last week in November. Everyone was nervous in our house now. At table, we children exchanged glances, kicked each other, and spoke of meaningless things. You could cut the strained silence.

"How is the silver cream pot coming that you're making for Lady Frankland, Paul?" Rachel asked.

"Well, my dear. Though the interior finish is not yet to my liking."

"She'll have little use for a cream pot," Grandmother put in. "A silver rum tankard would better suit her."

"Now, Mother, 'tis better to be kind than cantankerous," Father chided.

"I'm an old lady and find more pleasure in being cantankerous," she said.

"I got the new ribbons for Frances's bonnet today," Rachel said.

"Wonderful." Father beamed. "I can't wait to see you in it, Frances."

My sister screwed up her face. "Shan't wear it."

"Now, now, Lamb, Rachel has gone through a lot of trouble for your new frippery. And I, a lot of expense," Father said.

"Amos is coming tonight, Father." Debby dropped this into the conversation like a ham bone into a pot of stew.

Everyone fell silent. We were on dangerous ground now. Amos had become a cohort of my father's. He ran with the Sons. My father found him a good learner, an avid devotee of my father's principles. When he came to visit of an evening, he'd end up in the kitchen talking solemnly with my father. Debby was hard put to get him back into the parlor.

"Good, good." My father rubbed his hands. "Always glad to see the boy. Reminds me of myself when I was that age. Did I ever tell you children how, when I was a lad, I and my friends founded a bell ringers' association? One evening a week we rang the bells at North Church for two hours."

"You told us," we all chorused.

"Tell me," Rachel begged.

We looked at her. She wanted to keep the conversation chatty. She wanted us to talk about anything but what we were all dying to talk about. *Why, she feels slighted,* I thought. *So then, Father hasn't told her about his activities.*

Father launched into his story about ringing bells and drawing up a covenant and making a government with his friends for their association.

"You made a government?" Rachel was aghast.

"Yes," Father said. "It was a sacred covenant. We believed in the rule of law, self-government, and a majority vote."

"At thirteen?" Rachel was dumbfounded.

"It's the founding principle of New England, dear," Father said.

Rachel tightened her lips. I thought she looked frightened. "I think tomorrow I and the girls will visit their mother's grave at Old Granary," she said. "Paul, would you care to accompany us?"

My brother declined. "Thank you, ma'am, but I'm to help Father in the shop."

"Don't you think the little ones are too young?" Father asked.

"Respect for the dead. It's another founding principle of New England," Rachel said.

Their eyes met. Father looked pleased rather than surprised at her display of mettle. Grandmother looked disappointed. She would rather have had them disagree.

The next day at Old Granary, while my sisters were playing amongst the gravestones, showing a decided disrespect for the dead, Rachel drew me aside and asked me to tell her about my father. And his activities.

Chapter Five

*W*HEN," Rachel asked me, "did your father start doing things against the king?"

We were in a corner of the Old Granary grave-yard. A high stone wall sealed it off from the street, but I could hear the *clip-clop* of horses' hooves on cobblestone, the talk of passersby. Frances, Mary, and Elizabeth were running and playing in the distance. Debby was home making a raisin cake for when Amos came this evening.

"He doesn't do things against the king, Rachel."

"If we are to be friends, Sarah, I would have honesty between us."

I said naught.

"Your father is in the Sons of Liberty. They do things against the king."

I looked at her. It sounded so grievous when she put it in such words. "I can't speak of my father's activities. We've all promised him not to."

"His mother told me about the tea ships. And how he plans to keep watch. None of you are surprised when he leaves the house in the middle of the night. Why does no one think to tell me?"

"We supposed he told you before you wed."

"Oh, I knew about the crowd of hundreds that assembled in front of your house by torchlight on the first anniversary of the massacre. But I thought that was because he was popular with the common folk. And I knew of the punch bowl he made in honor of those who went against the king for the Townshend Acts. But I thought that was because he was just a good silversmith."

I stared at her sadly.

"I mind that I was lying to myself," she said. "Wasn't I?"

I nodded yes.

"I never asked, until lately. Do you know what he said?"

"No."

"He said, 'There, there, dear, don't worry your head about it.' "

She took out a square of cotton and blew her nose. I wished I'd stayed home to make raisin cake with Debby.

"Tell me, Sarah," she begged. "I won't give him grief about it. I just need to know. And I won't tell him you told me. I promise."

But I dared not. I swallowed and stared at her, very much in misery. I closed my eyes for a minute and prayed. *Mama, help me,* I prayed silently. *What am I to do now?*

And then I had a thought. No, it was more like a revelation. I did not question it. Sitting in the midst of a graveyard, right in front of Mama's stone with the skull and crossbones on it, why would I question it?

But it was absolutely brilliant. I was proud of myself.

"Why don't you ask Doctor Warren?" I said.

She looked at me. "What?"

"Doctor Warren. Why don't you ask him? He knows everything Father is about. And he's most amiable. I'm sure he'd tell you what you want to know. He's coming to sup tonight, isn't he?"

She blew her nose. "Yes. Thank you, Sarah. I think I will. I'm sorry. I shouldn't have asked you. Of course you can't betray your father's secrets. And you were right about Elizabeth. Now let's attend to Mary."

I smiled. Elizabeth had stopped wetting the bed since Ruffles was allowed back in the house. We gathered the little girls in, and Rachel had them stand before the headstone of the dead Mary.

"What do you see?" she asked my sister Mary, who was burying her face against my skirts.

"A headstone," the child answered.

"Yes. And it says, 'Here lies Mary. Angel of the Lord. Born March 31, 1764, died, April 30, 1765.' Here, touch the engraving."

Little Mary reached to touch the stone, carefully.

"This stone is not for you," Rachel said firmly. "This is for the dead Mary. She lies here, in peace. You only have the same name. It doesn't mean you will die. You are going to live to be a grand old lady."

Mary eyed her. "Like Grandmother?"

"Grander," Rachel said.

"Do you promise?"

"I promise," Rachel said. "Just because you have the same name as someone doesn't mean you'll die as they did. Look at Sarah. She has your mother's name and she isn't afraid of dying. Are you, Sarah?"

"She spells it different," Frances put in.

Rachel looked at me.

"Mama spelled it S-A-R-A," I explained. "I added an H."

"To what aim?" Rachel asked.

"To be grand," I said. But I was lying. I spelled it different so I wouldn't die as Mama had. I understood Mary's fears only too well.

"Sarah knows she and your mama are two different people," Rachel explained to Mary. "And you and first Mary are two different people. Do you understand?"

"I want to spell it dif'rent," Mary said. She was still afraid. And bargaining.

"You can't," Rachel said. "There is only one way to spell Mary. But what would you think if we called her First Mary and you Second Mary?"

Mary thought that would be fine. So fine that her round little face beamed, showing dimples. "I'm Second Mary," she said, jumping up and down. "You must call me Second Mary, all of you."

We left the graveyard promising we would. But I still wished I'd stayed home with Debby to make raisin cake.

THAT NIGHT Doctor Warren came to sup. As usual my little sisters climbed all over him.

"Doctor Warren, Doctor Warren, I'm now Second Mary," my sister told him. "You must call me Second Mary."

"Indeed, I will. But why?"

"So I won't be First Mary. And die!"

Debby and Paul laughed. But Doctor Warren didn't. He hugged her close. "You shan't die, Second Mary. Not if I have anything to say about it."

Of course, Frances must be paid mind to, then. She waited her turn. She read to him out of a primer. "I'm getting a new bonnet and dress," she told him.

"And you shall be the most beautiful lady in Boston. I can't wait to see you in it," he told her.

Elizabeth pushed her way in. "I don't wet the bed anymore," she told him.

"You're my fine big girl," he said. And he gave her some maple sugar out of his pocket.

"You've done wonderful things with the children, Rachel," Warren told her after supper.

Debby and I were clearing the dishes. Grandmother had gone to bed. Father smiled contentedly. "She's my dear girl," he said.

He and Warren stayed late in the parlor talking. Paul was with them. More and more of late Father was allowing Paul to sit in on these sessions.

Debby had gone out with Amos. I sat in the kitchen with Rachel. She was working on a crewel bedcover and I on a new apron. Finally, the meeting in the parlor broke up.

"Good night, friend," Father said to Warren. "Paul, will you see him out? Rachel, come to bed. It's late."

"You go up. I'll be along. I want to wrap my bread dough for the morning."

She then told me and Paul to go to bed, too. She would see Warren out and lock the door. And I knew she was going to ask him about Father's activities.

We went upstairs. But I crept down again. I

hovered there on the stairway. I could not see them, but I could hear their voices. And see the long flickering shadows cast by the candle between them at the kitchen table. They spoke in low tones.

I heard Warren telling her how the tradesmen and artisans had started the Sons of Liberty back in '65 when banks and merchants were failing. And merchants couldn't pay the duties England demanded.

In low, patient tones, he reassured her.

He did not belittle her fears. He listened. Warren always could listen well. It was part of being a doctor.

I heard him tell her how Father had distinguished himself doing the drawings for the Great Illumination in '66. "They were hung on the Commons," he said. "They were most inspiring. We've been through much together. Especially when the king last sent troops here, in the time of the massacre. Your husband is much esteemed by the common man and the gentry alike. He has friends of all persuasions. All trust him."

"I fear the Green Dragon meetings," she was

telling him. "I fear that place has become a nest of sedition. And what is being hatched will bring us all bad cess."

He becalmed her. "We are not men of violence," he said. "Do you know me as such, Rachel?"

Her laugh was soft. "No. But this business with the tea ships. Won't it lead to violence?"

"No. And I can promise you that, Rachel. We are thinking men, who only want their rights restored as Englishmen. We do not practice sedition. Do you know how many of the sixteen members of the Long Room Club, to which your husband belongs, are Harvard graduates?"

"No."

"Eleven," he said. "We will not condone violence."

Then she spoke. "You are so good with the children. And what of your own, then?"

"I miss them, sorely. I don't get the chance to see them as much as I'd like."

"And is there no woman, then, who captures your fancy, Doctor Warren? Half the women in Boston consider you a desirable catch."

His laugh was low and throaty. "Mayhap I do not wish to be caught, Rachel," he said.

I went up the stairs to bed. They had become fast friends. I did not know if that was a good thing or a bad thing. But I did know this. It was my doing.

FATHER MADE his first ride on the last day of November that year of '73. The *Dartmouth* had tied up at Griffin's Wharf on the twenty-eighth. The owner was ordered, on peril, not to unload her.

Father kissed Rachel good-bye. "I'm off to deliver letters to neighboring seaports to warn them that other tea ships may try to drop anchor," he said.

Rachel caught my eye and smiled. I minded that her face was white and set, that she was still frightened. But that she was more purposeful, too, as she readied the food for his saddlebags. She had gained some assurance, thanks to Doctor Warren.

Father kissed us, called us his lambs, then, booted and spurred, he led Militia through the streets for his first ride.

We did not know it was his first, until he made his second.

———

HE DID THAT on the seventeenth of December.

On the sixteenth none of us went to school.

My little sisters and I all went to dame school, run by Mrs. Tisdale. Most girls finished their education at age eight, but Father was not one to think it was sufficient for his girls only to be able to make their mark on paper.

I would go until Mrs. Tisdale thought me learned in my sums, my geography, my French, and my reading, as Debby had done. Then I would learn the womanly arts at home. As Debby was supposed to be doing. When anyone could make her.

On the sixteenth, Grandmother asserted herself and would not allow us out of the house. Rachel agreed with her.

The day before, the *Beaver* and the *Eleanor* dropped anchor at Griffin's Wharf, next to the *Dartmouth*. Now it drizzled a cold rain. Boston was in a frenzy.

"The ships must unload their cargo in twenty-six days or they are liable for seizure. Those are the rules," Paul told us.

Father had stood guard last night. We expected him to come through the door at any moment.

Paul kept a paper in the kitchen on which he marked off the days since the *Dartmouth* had arrived.

"Eighteen," he counted the morning of the sixteenth.

"Sit down and have breakfast," Debby said.

"No time. I'll be late. Master Pitts will be angry."

"No school," Grandmother said. "Not today. Not for any of you."

The girls squealed in delight. Paul didn't. "I have to go. Master Pitts is taking us to the meeting at Old South this afternoon. He says it's our patriotic duty to go. Rachel?" He looked at her, begging.

"This once I agree with your grandmother," she said. "There are thousands assembled. It will become a mob."

"Father said I could go," Paul argued.

Rachel was about to reply, when Father came through the door. We jumped up and crowded around him, asking questions.

"Quiet, all of you. Sit down, my lambs. Debby, fetch me some bread, meat, and rum."

Father took his place at the table. "Now, my lambs, I am going to break my rule of silence about my activities. You all deserve to know what is acting. But you must listen and learn."

He smiled across the table at Rachel. She smiled back, weakly. I supposed she'd told him of her conversation with Doctor Warren, and how he explained my father's activities to her.

"The tea on these ships is good bohea. And cheap. Ten shillings a pound. How much does tea go for, children?"

"Twenty shillings a pound," we all recited.

Father often turned news from the streets into lessons.

"Good. Now I put forth to you that Parliament thinks we can't resist this cheap price. So they've put a tax of threepence a pound on it and cut our merchants out of the market."

We all listened dutifully.

"More than a thousand chests of tea have been sent to Charleston, Philadelphia, New York, and here. New York and Philadelphia forced the consignees to refuse to receive it. Those ships' captains have turned around and gone home."

Father smiled. "Who can tell me what a consignee is?"

"It's an agent who handles the sale," I said.

Father smiled. "Good, good. Now, the Hutchinsons have gotten themselves appointed consignees for Boston's tea. Who can tell me what a commission is?"

"Money," Frances piped in.

Father took a gulp of rum. "Well, Hutchinson wants his commission. So he refuses to allow the ships to go back to England until he has a receipt from the customhouse declaring the duty has been paid. He has run off to his house in Milton."

"And now what?" Rachel asked.

"Mr. Rotch, who owns the *Dartmouth,* has gone thence to beg him to allow his ship to clear Boston Harbor. How many miles is it to Milton and back, Paul?"

"Fourteen." But Paul's voice was sullen.

Father nodded and sighed. "So now we wait. And we vote this afternoon on what to do if Governor Hutchinson won't let the ships return home."

"And what will that vote likely be?" Rachel's voice was clear and firm.

Father looked across the table at her. "The ships have been moved to the inner harbor. They are secured by long cables to Griffin's Wharf. This evening they will swing down with the tide.

We hope for the rain to cease. And we vote. Do we want a full moon or a half-moon to appear over the chimney pots of Boston tonight? Well, Elizabeth, what do you think?"

"Full!" she shouted.

"And for what purpose?" Father asked.

"So you can see," Elizabeth said.

"Smart girl. So I shall vote for a full moon, then."

"You can't vote for a moon," Frances said. And she ran and put her arms around him.

Father hugged her. "Then you pray for one for me, will you? And you take Second Mary and Elizabeth to the other room and pop some corn for us."

The little girls left.

"What if Hutchinson says no?" Rachel's voice was less firm.

"Then, love, we do what we must do."

"Bah!" Grandmother put in. "Hutchinson will never let those ships go. The Hutchinsons are greedy. Always were."

"Do you fear bloodshed, Paul?" Rachel asked.

"Not a life will be lost, not a drop of blood shed, not a man hurt, I promise you," Father told her. "Doctor Warren and I have agreed. There will be no mean movement for private revenge."

"Can I go to school, Father?" Paul asked. "Master Pitts is going to take us to witness the voting."

"I need you here," Father said. "I'm going to nap now. Doctor Warren is stopping by to fetch me. I want to be wakened at five. We'll need some lampblack and old blankets. Debby, Amos may be stopping by, too."

Debby came alive. "Amos is going with you?"

"If Amos can go so can I," Paul said.

Father said no. He took Paul aside, put his arm around him, and spoke softly. By the time he finished whatever he said, Paul was convinced that staying home was his special mission. This was Father's way. He could charm us into doing his will.

The rain stopped by two and a clear wind rose. At four-thirty we heard footsteps out on the cobblestones. Then a knock on the door.

It was Doctor Warren, tall and fair, blue-eyed and dressed as immaculately as for a ball. Amos was with him.

"Clearance for the tea ships was refused," Doctor Warren told us.

He greeted us all, in turn, with a special word

for each. The children crowded around him, as always, to fish maple sugar out of his pockets. He took Elizabeth on his lap. I gave him a cup of chocolate. Debby was in a far corner of the kitchen with Amos.

Paul went to wake Father, who then came into the kitchen. When Doctor Warren gave him the news about the tea ships, they embraced.

"Get the lampblack," Father said to Paul.

Then we all watched while Father and Doctor Warren blackened their faces and hands. There was much teasing of Doctor Warren, because he was always so scrupulously clean. And much merriment, as if they were making ready for a Pope's Day parade.

In the corner, apart from everyone else, Debby blackened Amos's face. Her own face was set and white, but she showed nary a tear. Then, when Amos was quite blackened, she stood on tiptoe and kissed his cheek.

I envied my sister at that moment. She was ages ahead of me. I was a child in comparison.

And I felt very much the child, very small and frightened when they went out into the early evening cold. We wished them Godspeed, and Paul closed and bolted the door. It was a quarter of six, the December sun had set early, it seemed.

"Now we're all going to play some games before supper," he told the small children. "Then you're off to bed."

I noticed that he never allowed his musket to be far from his side as he amused the younger ones.

We ate supper. Elizabeth's prayers for a full moon were answered because one rose that evening. Grandmother went to bed. Rachel sat mending. Debby took up crewelwork, and I roasted some apples on the hearth.

The night grew quiet, except for an occasional voice outside or a dog barking. All usual sounds. The children went to bed. I dozed. Finally Rachel put her mending aside.

"I think we should all go to bed. Sarah? Debby? Paul?"

"I'll sleep here," Paul said.

She gave him no argument. We went to bed.

Debby and I shared a room. We undressed, facing away from each other. I turned to see my sister, a tall, straight figure in her flannel nightdress, looking out the window.

"The sky glows in the direction of Griffin's Wharf," she said. "This night is special."

"Why?"

She shook her head, unable to explain. "Enough to say it will live in memory forever."

I became annoyed. How like Debby to act as if she were privy to some special secret. Though likely Amos had told her everything. But she acted so smug I wanted to pinch her.

She opened the window. Cold air rushed in. "I can hear something," she said.

"What?" Though shivering, I put my head out the window. "I don't hear anything. And the sky isn't glowing. You're fancying things."

"No, I hear a sound like the chopping of wood."

"Why can't I hear it?"

"Because you don't have someone out there." She closed the window. "Let's go to bed."

I felt like saying "bah," like Grandmother.

"Aren't you afraid for Amos?" I asked from under my quilt.

"No. They know what they're about, those men out there."

She blew out the candle. The wind rattled against the window. I thought of Father, wearing rags, his face blackened, doing God knew what in the bitter cold. And I felt ashamed because I was frightened. Then I minded that Rachel was frightened, too. But not Debby.

"Debby," I said, "you make me angry most of the time. Do you know that?"

"Yes," she said.

"But tonight when I saw you with Amos, it came to me. You've grown up. You've gone your way since Mama died. All on your own."

"I've had to," she said.

"I wish I could be brave like you."

"It comes when you're smitten with some-one."

"Do you think I'll ever be?"

"What? Smitten? Or brave?"

"Either."

"Yes," she said sleepily.

Then why isn't Rachel brave? I wondered. But I didn't ask. I didn't feel as if I could betray Rachel's confidences.

In the morning I came downstairs to find Debby crisp and cheerful, helping Rachel pre-pare breakfast. Rachel looked ragged in compar-ison. Grandmother was having her tea, sipping it from her saucer as she was wont to do.

I slipped into my chair. "Grandmother, how could you drink tea this day?"

She grinned wickedly. "Men are all fools. Each generation must run off when the drums beat for volunteers. My grandfather, Captain Richard Pattishall from Maine, went off to chase pirates. The last thing he told my grandmother was that he'd be back directly. The Indians butchered him while he slept on his own ship as it anchored off Pemaquid."

Mary began to sniffle and cry.

A loud bang from the hearth made me jump. "Stop that, Mother Revere!" Rachel snapped.

Everyone stared.

Rachel approached the table, hands on her hips. "You tell these children so many horrible stories. No wonder they are filled with fear."

"I tell them truths," Grandmother said. "It's good for them to know truths."

"Sometimes it isn't," Rachel said. "And this is one of those times. So drink your tea if you must, but no horror stories this morning, if you please."

Grandmother fell silent. I got up to help with breakfast. Then Father came in.

Everyone froze. Little Elizabeth screamed.

Though she had seen him blacken his face, the sight of him, his torn coat, his hair in disarray, frightened her.

"Hello, my lambs." And he held out his arms. "It's me. Come here, Elizabeth. I was out playing games. Did you pray for that full moon? We had it."

The little girls ran to him. Rachel stood there, spoon in hand, mouth open. "Paul, you're home!"

"Of course I am. I told you I would be."

Rachel brought him a soft wet rag and wiped his face. Then she kissed him.

"Did you bring me any tea?" Grandmother asked.

"Nary a fistful, Mother. None of the Mohawks took so much as a spoonful for themselves. Those who felt so inclined were persuaded otherwise."

"Mohawks?" Rachel asked.

He sat down, wearily. "Yes. You see, family, it seems the tea ships were boarded by Indians last night. They dumped eighteen thousand pounds' worth of tea into the water. After breaking open the chests with hatchets."

I caught Debby's eye. So she *had* heard the chopping of wood. I shivered. It was eerie.

"They say the baneful weed is marking the edge of high tide on beaches as far south as Nantasket this morning," Father said.

"You *dumped the tea?*" Rachel was aghast.

"No, my dear, the Indians did."

"What of Amos?" Debby asked lightly.

"As right as rain, daughter."

"Eat." Rachel put his food down in front of him. "And then you'll have a wash and to bed." She was angry.

He commenced to eat. We all watched. "I'm about starved," he said, "but I can't rest. Paul, saddle Militia."

"You're *not* going out," Rachel said.

"My dear, I must. An account of what's been done is this minute being drawn up by the Committee of Correspondence. It must be brought, immediately, to Philadelphia and New York."

"Let someone else bring it," Rachel said. "You need your sleep."

"Sleep I can do without. They are in need of my services. There will be plenty of time for sleeping. Paul?"

"I'm going, Father." And he went out the door.

Father took Rachel into the parlor after breakfast and closed the door. But the sound of their voices came through the door, in low argument.

The children had gone out to play. Grandmother dozed by the hearth. I helped Debby clean up.

"She's not happy," Debby said of a sudden.

I looked at her. "She fears for him. Can you lay blame for that?"

She shrugged.

"Not everyone can be brave like you, Debby."

"Men get killed falling from ships' masts," she said. "They get kicked by horses, they drown at sea. Boston's had the pox and fires."

"Then there's enough that can befall us without looking for it," I said.

"She'll have to learn. There are worse things than death."

"Worse?" I gaped.

She nodded. "Do you recollect how he was after Mama died? All curled up inside himself? How we feared for his mind?"

"Yes."

"He's happy now."

"Because of Rachel," I reminded her.

"True. But that won't last if she keeps him from defending the public liberty. You know how Father believes in it."

It was the first time I'd heard his beliefs put into words. I felt jealous that Debby was the one to do it.

"You should tell her," she said. "She's taken to you."

"Tell her what?"

The door of the parlor opened then, and they came out.

Debby moved closer to me. "That she must accept him as he is. Or it will all be ruined. Do you want that? Do you want them to have a marriage like his friend Isaiah Thomas?"

Thomas was the publisher of the *Massachusetts Spy,* a wild rebel sheet that appealed to the lower classes. My father did drawings for it.

"His wife can't abide what her husband is printing against the king. She's frightened. She runs with Tory men to save herself."

"Rachel wouldn't do such," I whispered.

"Who knows what a frightened woman will do?"

"She'll be all right," I insisted. "Doctor Warren has talked to her."

She looked at me. "What mean you by that?"

"She asked me about Father's activities. I couldn't tell her. So I suggested she speak with Doctor Warren. She did. And he put her at ease. I know she's still worried, but she'll be all right," I said again.

"Dear God"—Debby raised her eyes to the ceiling—"you've let the fox into the henhouse."

Of course, I did not take her meaning. How could I?

Father went upstairs. Debby moved away from me. Rachel came into the kitchen blowing her nose. "He must have cheese and corn bread," she directed. "And a slab of ham. You slice it, Debby. Careful, don't cut your finger. Sarah, get some of those apples you roasted last evening. They're dry, but they'll do until he can get to an inn for a leg of lamb, country bread, and some flip."

I moved to do her bidding, but my mind was numb. Would fear make Rachel like Mary Dill, wife of Isaiah Thomas? Was *that* why Mary had taken to running with Tory men?

Father came down, booted and in clean

clothing. I handed him his spurs. He buckled them on. Through the windows we could see Paul leading Militia. She was restless, eager to be off. You could see her puffs of breath in the cold air.

Good-byes were swift. "I'll sleep in the saddle," he told Rachel. "Riding Militia is like being in a featherbed."

And then he went out the door into the cold December air. He mounted his horse, leaned down to say something to Paul, then waved at us and rode away.

On his second ride.

We stood, the three of us, watching him through the window that looked out on the yard.

Then Rachel gave a great sigh. "Well, who wants to come to market with me?"

"I'll go," I offered. "Shall I get the little ones?"

"No, I'll watch them," Debby offered. "You two go off. Why don't you get some fresh lemons, Rachel? I hear they had some off a ship from the Indies at market yesterday. I'll make a lemon cake."

The next day Debby told me that Amos told her that one "Indian" had gotten home to find his shoes were full of tea. He put it into a glass bottle. And labeled it "tea party." Debby swore me to secrecy about who he was. But I suppose it is all right to say it now. His name was Thomas Melville.

Chapter Six

*C*HRIST'S EPISCOPAL was ringing its royal peal of eight bells. It was the twenty-fifth of December. A Saturday.

Father wasn't home from his ride yet. We had no word of him. On the streets they were already singing a ditty about the tea party.

They sang about "bold Revere" and "our Warren."

They were the only ones identified in the tea dumping.

In our house we were harried. We worried for Father. We heard rumor on the streets that Boston was going to have to raise eighteen thousand pounds to pay the East India Company for the tea.

The citizens were divided in opinion over the whole business. Some said it was an act of out-and-out lawlessness. Others applauded the action. In church last Sunday there had been a fight.

We were Congregationalist. We went to New Brick, otherwise known as the Cockerel, so named because of the huge brass weathervane of a rooster on the steeple.

"There was a majesty to the act," Thomas Young stood up and said.

Peter Wendell held that it added another branch to the liberty tree.

"Another branch to hang us on," yelled John Apley. "I tremble when I think of the dire consequences."

Church was never dull, for all the long sermons. Scandal, politics, and local events were always discussed. But now feelings were running wild.

"And where is the bold Paul?" Apley pointed a finger at us. "Fled to more peaceful climes?"

My brother stood up. "My father is one appointed by the committee to visit towns with a formal announcement of the tea action." His voice was strong and clear. "All town committees must now unite."

I was so proud of Paul!

"Aye," Apley scolded. "And what if other towns don't back us? Has Paul the Bold given thought to that?"

It was then that Rachel grabbed my brother's arm, whispered to the children, and we all filed out. Even Grandmother. But she and Rachel had high words about the leaving.

"We own pews in that church." Grandmother yelled. "And you let them frighten us out."

That was on the nineteenth. Now, on the twenty-fifth, they still were not speaking.

It was morning. The reason Christ's Episcopal was ringing its bells was because it was Christmas. Grandmother had us all up early, cooking a feast with vengeance.

She knew Rachel, true Congregationalist that she was, did not hold with Christmas.

This was her way of getting back. We could not have been in a worse situation in our house.

Rachel came downstairs and into the kitchen. She looked spent. I knew she wasn't sleeping nights. I heard her walking about. She was worried, but then she had reason to be.

Grandmother and Debby knew it, too. I'd caught them whispering about her several times.

A line had been drawn in our house, with Debby and Grandmother on one side, I and Rachel on the other. The children ran back and forth across it, sensing they could profit from the division in the family.

My brother, in the manner of all men, pretended it did not exist.

"What's all this?" Rachel asked. She saw me rolling pie dough, Debby chopping nuts for stuffing, Elizabeth on a floor licking mincemeat out of a bowl, and Mary and Frances molding newly made butter. There was a saddle of mutton cooking on the hearth.

"It's Christmas," Grandmother said. "Why else church bells on Saturday?"

"Sarah, do we have coffee?" Rachel asked. "Those bells afflict my head." She got headaches from the damp night air.

"Those bells are beautiful," Debby said dreamily. "The other night Amos and I heard them clear across the harbor."

"And what were you and Amos doing clear across the harbor?" Rachel asked.

"He was making a delivery for his master. I went with him."

"Those bells dispel demons," Grandmother said.

I had kept coffee brewing for Rachel. I got some now, with corn bread and some slices of ham on a plate. I cleared a place at the table. "Sit," I said.

"Would that they could dispel demons," Rachel said. "Must you pound so, Debby?"

"The walnuts must be crushed for the stuffing."

"What are we stuffing?"

"Whatever Paul brings from market. There's plenty of wild fowl."

Rachel sipped her coffee. Her mind cleared. "Since when do Congregationalists keep Christmas?"

"Since my husband, Appolos Rivoire, left the persecutions of Huguenot France and brought the custom with him," Grandmother said.

Rachel knew that was an embellishment. We all did. Though the reason for his leaving was persecution, our French Protestant grandfather was sent first to Holland, then to Guernsey, where he set sail for America in 1716.

Grandmother made it sound as if the Catholic king of France personally brandished his sword, driving Grandfather to the point of sail.

"Christmas smacks of the selfsame idolatry and brimstone from which your husband fled," Rachel reminded her.

"Bah!" piped Grandmother. "We could use a little idolatry and brimstone in the Cockerel. Liven things up."

Rachel yawned. "I would say they were sufficient lively."

"And who's to say we Congregationalists are right in *not* keeping Christmas?" Grandmother asked. "Are we of a higher order because we have Hutchinsons in our church? Or Hancocks?"

"They're a credit to us," Rachel said.

"Bah! I never liked those Hancocks for all their money. John's uncle was new-risen money. And his aunt Lydia takes on airs. Just because Copley did her in pastels."

"Copley wants to paint my husband's portrait," Rachel told her.

"Who needs a portrait?" Grandmother asked. "Will it put food on the table?"

"We have food aplenty," Rachel returned. "Paul is a good provider."

"Better Copley should pay him for the silver picture frame he fashioned for him."

I could abide it no longer. "Stop it! Both of you!" I yelled. "I liked it better when you weren't speaking."

I'd been turning the side of mutton on the fire. Everyone stared at me. I dropped the long fork with a clatter and ran from the room.

Little Elizabeth started to cry. Rachel picked her up and held her in her lap. I hid in the parlor, ashamed of my outburst, wishing Father were here. I don't know what all would have happened if the door had not opened then, admitting a gust of cold air and my brother.

"Aren't these the handsomest partridges you've ever seen?" He held up three. "There's fowl in great plenty at market."

Everyone exclaimed over the partridges. Elizabeth stopped crying. From the parlor, I saw Rachel get up.

"I must needs go out."

"Where, on Christmas?" Grandmother asked.

Rachel reached for her cloak. "To market. I don't keep Christmas, remember?"

"We've all we need here," Grandmother argued.

"I'm meeting a friend," Rachel said. "She needs me to help pick out some silk for a new gown."

"What friend?" Grandmother asked.

Rachel smiled, going out the door. "Isn't a woman allowed a friend or two from before her marriage, Deborah? I'm sure you can keep things in order here. I don't seem to be needed."

"It's crowded at market today," Paul said. "Two ships just dropped anchor from the West Indies."

"I'll get some fresh lemons for tea," Rachel said. And she went out the door.

"Sarah!" Grandmother summoned me.

"Yes, Grandmother?"

"Get your cloak." She reached into a stoneware jar on a shelf. "Ships from the West Indies mean pimentos. I require some."

I took the shillings. "What do we need pimentos for, Grandmother?"

Paul said something about plucking the feathers from the partridges, took a kettle of hot water, and went into the yard. Grandmother waited until the door closed behind him.

"Follow her," she whispered.

"I'll not spy on Rachel," I whispered savagely.

"You'll do as you're told," Debby said. "She's sneaked out twice to see this Tory friend of hers."

"How do you know her friend is Tory? She simply has fears since the tea was dumped."

"For Father," she sneered, "or for Doctor Warren?"

"I think you're mean, Debby. You know they're for Father. I think you're under Grandmother's influence too much. Half of Boston fears what Parliament will do to punish us."

"I don't."

"Well, mayhap that's because Amos's name isn't being bandied about in a ballad."

"Hush," Grandmother said. "No goodwife runs about as she's been doing of late. Friends from before her marriage, indeed." She gripped my arm. "Go! Just tell me whom she meets, that's all I want to know. We must be careful. Don't you think your father's life is in danger?"

Then she pushed me out the door.

I went out into the cold, sobered by the

thought. Would Rachel run to Tory friends now? She *was* frightened, yes. But she had every right to be. And look at the way Grandmother had pushed Christmas at her. If she did that to me and I didn't like Christmas, I'd walk out, too.

Of course, I liked Christmas. I wished we Congregationalists kept it in our church, with greens and music. Why should the Episcopalians have all the sport?

ON MARKET DAY, there was no getting through the streets of the North End. I gathered my cloak around me, bent my head to the wind, and set myself to the task.

It was no trifling business. The streets were mobbed with ladies and gentlemen in fine frippery; apprentices in leather aprons; small nigra boys with brooms and rags trying to solicit chimneys to sweep; sailors in tarred pigtails; bully boys, oystermen with their catches in sacks on their backs; and just plain harlots.

"Oil, fine Seneca oil here," a peddler hawked. He led a horse pulling a small cart of stoneware jars. A quack, Doctor Warren would call him. The Seneca oil came from Pennsylvania Indians. They got it from some kind of springs, and it was supposed to be good for rheumatism. It smelled horrible.

Carts rattled all around. They lumbered in with produce from the countryside all day.

The smells, sounds, and the music could easily distract one from her own personage. And so one must be careful of pickpockets.

The pungent odor of tar burning in barrels to heat the market mingled with the smell of herbs, fish, hay, animals, freshly imported coffee, and baking bread.

The sounds were those of gulls crying overhead, the lapping of water in the harbor, workmen hammering, people bargaining, church bells ringing, and wagon wheels creaking. And there was always music. This day some musicians were playing tunes on both a harpsichord and violin.

Once inside the market, it took only a moment for me to adjust my eyes to the dimness and special sights. I walked up and down the main aisle, trying to spot Rachel.

There were all kinds of oddments in market, everything from a polar bear on a chain to a doll dressed in the latest London fashion.

This day many booths were advertising exotic coffees. Coffee had become all the rage now, with the dumping of the tea. And there were several booths with signs. One praised "Rye Coffee," another decried "Poisonous Bohea." My eye was attracted to a sign that read:

Ladies, Save America
from the Danger of Tyranny!
Show the British that
American patriotism extends even to
the Fair Sex.
Come, partake of our exotic coffee
fresh from the West Indies.
Tea drinking will be paid for by
the blood of your sons.

There, on a rude brick hearth, the proprietor was brewing coffee that gave off a fragrance to entice the most ardent tea drinker.

And there sat Rachel, showing the British that American patriotism extended even to the Fair Sex. She was sipping coffee.

The only problem was her companion was a Tory.

She was sitting with none other than Lady Frankland, otherwise known as Agnes Surriage, the woman Grandmother hated.

I ducked behind a post, watching them for a

minute. They were deep in conversation. Agnes was dressed in the height of fashion. She wore a cloak of blue velvet trimmed with ermine. Just outside the booth, I saw her nigra boy waiting and holding her fluffy little dog.

Rachel looked so plain in comparison. But there was no lack of warmth between the women. Indeed, they chatted like old friends.

Then I recollected that they were. Hadn't it been Agnes who'd first sent Rachel by? Because she'd heard my father was in need of a new love?

I minded what Grandmother had told us about Agnes. She'd been a serving girl, barefoot, scrubbing a floor at an inn in Marblehead when Sir Harry had met her. He'd taken her off with him on the spot, brought her to his mansion in Boston, and told people he was going to educate her.

People whispered about them. Sir Harry didn't care. He took her on a trip to England. Then to Portugal. There they witnessed an earthquake. It frightened Sir Harry into marrying her, Grandmother said. And he brought her back to Boston and bought the old Clark house for her. A mansion just off North Square.

It had eight hundred and sixty-five pieces of

wood in the mahogany floor. And was supposed to be more elegant than any in town. Still people wouldn't speak to Agnes.

My father had made a silver tea set for her. He and my mother always greeted her on the street.

Sir Harry died in 1770. Agnes lived in the house alone now, with her parrot, her small fluffy dog, and her nigra help.

She didn't care what people said anymore. She took satisfaction out of being a colorful character in Boston, a town with many colorful characters.

But she was still a Tory.

True, Sir Harry had been a decent sort. Father said he never even *looked* into kegs marked salt to see if merchants might be importing Madeira instead.

But that was before the tea dumping. Before the trouble with the stamps, even. No Tories were looked upon as decent sorts anymore.

I watched the two women a moment more. Agnes was the older, by years. Grandmother said Agnes had been a friend of Rachel's aunt, first. And that the friendship persisted when that aunt died.

My mother had once told me she had nary a woman friend, and how the wives of my father's cohorts in the Masons snubbed her. "Because I was never fancy enough for Abigail Adams or the like," she'd said.

My mother, I realized now, had always been lonely. I recollected the hurt in her voice as she'd said that. And so, standing there, I came to a decision.

If Rachel wanted this woman for a friend, she would suffer no grief from me. I would not tell Grandmother I'd seen them together. It would only spirit the old lady up against Rachel.

I would lie. I purchased the pimentos for Grandmother and rushed outside. I'd tell Grandmother simply that I'd seen Rachel sipping coffee in a booth.

"And what need does she have to go out of the house to sip coffee?" Grandmother would ask.

"To save America from tyranny," I would answer.

I was so busy mulling the matter over that I bumped right into a man. My package fell to the ground.

"Pardon me," he said.

"It was my fault, sir." I looked up into the face of Doctor Warren. And stood dumbstruck, like the mindless idiot I was.

He retrieved my package. "Sarah, did I hurt you?"

I assured him he had not.

"I've news of your father." He put a hand on my shoulder. "I've a dispatch from a friend in Philadelphia. Your father arrived there safely and proceeded to New York. He has been riding sixty-three miles a day and should soon be home."

"Oh, thank you, Doctor Warren. We were all grievous worried. Especially Rachel."

He frowned. "I know she doesn't sleep nights when he takes these rides of his. Mayhap I'll stop by this evening."

"Oh, do. She does so set store in what you say."

He came that evening. They adjourned to the parlor and for an hour at least he engaged her in conversation.

"What's he doing here when Father is away?" Debby asked.

"I invited him. To talk to Rachel. Likely he'll give her something to help her sleep."

"Hmmph," she said. "I hope you know what you're about. Are you sure you asked him here for *Rachel?*"

Again I didn't take her meaning. Or mayhap I didn't want to.

Two days later, Father came home.

"Militia is a joy to ride," he told us. "She is surefooted and nimble."

The sturdy sorrel mare looked no worse for wear as my brother led her to the barn.

In the kitchen, Father set down his saddlebags. Outside it was sleeting. Inside, the children had been quarrelsome all day. The room smelled of the damp clothing that hung on strung rope. Grandmother was napping in her room.

"How is my girl?" My father held out his arms to Rachel.

She stood across at the hearth stirring some soup. "Keeping." She straightened up and looked at him. "Your mother isn't speaking to me because yesterday when the sun favored us with its presence, I put some clothing on her gooseberry bushes in the yard. Mary and Elizabeth have been fighting for the last hour over a pull toy. Frances refuses to take her shoes off when she sleeps because she says the British are going to attack us for dumping the tea and we must be ready to run."

"Who told her such nonsense?" Father asked.

"I did," Debby spoke up, "the other day when she wouldn't behave. I didn't know it would frighten her so."

Rachel went on. "Paul wants to leave school. Isaiah Thomas has been around three times to ask you to do drawings for his new magazine. He's muddied my floor and befouled the air with his miserable pipe and sat here bemoaning the fact that his wife has threatened to go off on a jaunt with another man even to her eternal ruin. The only one I have no complaint against is Sarah. How was your trip, Paul?"

He beamed. "Whigs in both New York and Philadelphia say that we in Boston took proper action with the tea."

Rachel set down the spoon and burst into tears. "Oh, I'm so glad! To think that you bring us such news! And here I stand complaining like a fishwife."

"Here, my girl," said my father, and held out his arms.

Rachel ran into them. And everything was put to rights again in our house. Father was home.

Chapter Seven

*Y*OU WOULD THINK," Debby said, "that Rachel would be offended at least."

We rushed along Clark's Wharf to Father's shop. I carried his noon meal and Debby carried Paul's. Father was behind in his work. And on the fine days of spring, Debby and I had taken to bringing their noon repast to them. Paul had finally persuaded Father to allow him to leave North Writing to help in the shop.

Father had work in great plenty. Copper engravings. Some were of Captain Cook's voyage for a New York publisher. Others for Isaiah Thomas's *Royal American Magazine*.

It was one of those engravings of which Debby now spoke, a woman held down by a crowd of bullies as a doctor poured tea down her throat. The "doctor" was Lord Frederick North, the king's chief minister. The woman, of course, was a helpless America.

The woman was naked from the waist up.

People were saying that Rachel had posed for the woman. And Doctor Warren for the doctor.

"Rachel has decided to make sport of it," I said. "She says the accusations will go away if she does not give them credence."

"Are you sure she isn't languishing in the thought?"

"Debby!" I stopped. "How can you say such?"

"Did you see the look on his face the other night when the matter was brought up in jest? He blushed."

"And well he should! Isaiah Thomas's wife did the posing."

"He's not supposed to blush. He's a doctor."

"Well, he's a man, too, isn't he?"

She sighed. "It matters naught who posed for it, Sarah. It's what people think that counts."

"To me what matters is what's true, Debby. I

couldn't care a pig's tooth what people think. And you shouldn't, either."

"Are you saying we shouldn't care what people are saying about Rachel running off every Saturday afternoon to drink coffee with Lady Frankland?"

"Yes. Lady Frankland is an old friend. Rachel needs friends. Father's away so much these days."

"A *Tory* friend. Open your eyes, Sarah. Look around you. This great port is about to be closed by Parliament for what we did with the tea."

On the waterfront, two of His Majesty's ships had already dropped anchor. After June first, just two days away, not even a ferry would be allowed to cross the river to Charlestown.

Barges crowded the river now, needing berth. They brought supplies—flour, grain, foodstuffs, fuel. Families rushed by us, carrying furniture, children, even livestock in their wagons, to take the last of the ferries out to country homes. They feared riot and hunger. Wharves were crowded with merchants moving their ships and goods to Salem or Marblehead.

It had been like this since the thirteenth of

May, when the *Lively* arrived with the order from Parliament.

On the fourteenth, Father had ridden off again, to New York and Philadelphia. "Our worthy citizen, Mr. Paul Revere, is now well on his way with important letters to the southern colonies," the *Gazette* had reported.

He was gone twelve days. Twice in that time, Rachel had met Lady Frankland for coffee. I know because Grandmother made me follow her. I didn't tell Grandmother. But Rachel had been seen and someone told Debby. And Debby told her.

Father returned with good news. "New York is with us and against our port closing," he said. "Philadelphia will stand with us to the last extremity. They are laying the plans for a Continental Congress to discuss the plight of the colonies. Though they say we in Boston have a state of mind not sympathetic to law and order, as do Quakers."

Meantime, Parliament recalled Governor Hutchinson. And General Thomas Gage arrived on the seventeenth. He was commander in chief of the British forces in America.

"Any day now," Debby enunciated clearly, "any day, British troops will be landing."

Well I knew that. But with Debby it was always as if she were the only one who ever knew anything.

"This isn't the time for our stepmother to take coffee with a Tory friend."

The intensity of her stare was not lost on me. "What are you saying, Debby?"

"That Father must be told."

"What?"

"Don't play at being stupid. That Rachel is meeting with this woman."

"He knows," I said. "They confide in one another."

"Do they? Has he told her yet the extent of his political activities?"

"Doctor Warren has."

"Oh yes, how could I forget? The sage of Boston."

Her sarcasm went against the grain with me. "I think you oughtn't to badger Rachel so, Debby. You're picking on her. Aren't you glad she's made us a family again? Haven't we had enough turmoil?"

She tightened her lips. "All I know is that either you tell him today or I will."

She meant it. "Then I suppose you'll just have to do it. For I've no such intention."

"Very well, I will."

"I'd be careful, though. You don't know everything."

"What don't I know, pray? Enlighten me with your wisdom, little sister."

It was the way she had of saying "little sister" that galled me so. It just drove me to distraction. So I told her. "Rachel's going to have a child."

I heard her gasp. "You lie."

"And why should I? To what aim?"

"Who told you?"

"She did. Last time Father went away."

"And why wasn't I told?"

"Well, you haven't exactly been a friend to her, Debby. You or Grandmother. Anyway, Doctor Warren is supposed to tell us children tonight. When he comes for supper."

"Why Doctor Warren?"

"You know how Father is shy about making mention of such things."

She walked briskly, head down. "You see

nothing strange in her friendship with Doctor Warren? Doesn't it seem curious to you that they get on so?"

"He's a good friend of Father's. And true. And he's helped her understand Father's work. We owe him a debt."

"Indeed. Well, mayhap *you* do, Sarah, but I don't. And mayhap the reason you're always defending him is because you're so smitten with him yourself!"

And with that she ran on ahead. I followed slowly. Was she right about Doctor Warren and Rachel? Why could I not see it? And as for what she'd said about me being smitten with him, well, it was not the first time she had hinted such.

But it was the first time I had to admit to myself that she was right. I worshiped the man. But my feelings were pure.

She told Father that day about Rachel and Lady Frankland.

She did let him have his meal first. I'll give her that. We sat in the sunny shop with the windows open and the sounds and smells of the harbor coming in.

We admired a broadside Father had designed about the closing of our port. It was decorated with mourning bands, a crowned skull, and cross-bones.

"Take them and hand them out on the way home," my brother suggested. "Is it all right, Father?"

"I see no reason why not. Just don't approach any rabid Tories with them."

"We know no rabid Tories," I said.

"Yes we do," said Debby. "We know Lady Frankland."

All was quiet, but Father sensed something in the moment and spoke to my sister. "I don't think she's a rabid anything."

"I wouldn't be so sure about that, Father." And then she told him about Rachel meeting her.

Father remained calm. "Thank you for your concern, Debby."

"Is that all you have to say?"

"If Rachel is a friend to this woman, I'll not interfere."

"But she's a *Tory!*"

"If she's anything like her husband, none of us has anything to fear. Would that he were with us today. I know he'd oppose this port bill."

"Father! A Tory is a Tory."

"Not always," he said.

"How can you say that?"

"I can and I do. Some are our friends. Some will remain our friends. Many are confused about the turn things have taken. You and Amos are of a mind, daughter. You know what you are and what you stand for. With some people it is not so simple. Most people don't know how to feel. They have old ties, new concerns, family considerations."

"If this is the way of Lady Frankland, then all the more reason Rachel shouldn't see her."

"Lady Frankland is harmless," Father said. "She still has the heart of a barefoot scrubbing girl, for all her fancy living."

"I still say she bears watching," Debby said.

Father smiled. "Then Rachel can watch her."

Debby was furious. "How *can* you make sport of me?"

"I'm not making sport of you, Debby."

"Then what are you saying?"

"That I trust Rachel. That we must trust those we love."

My sister made a sound of contempt. No one said anything for a moment, then Father spoke. "You two girls are pulling apart," he said. "I don't like my lambs fighting."

"Well, she's such a little noodle head," Debby said of me. "She knew Rachel was meeting Lady Frankland and she said naught of it to you. Why don't you scold *her?*"

Father looked at me, his brown eyes taking my measure. "She's your sister," he said to Debby.

"That doesn't make her any less a noodle head."

Father sighed. Debby threw down the broadsides and stomped to the door. "Pass them out yourself," she said to Paul. But I knew—and I sensed Father knew, too—that she was saying it to him.

When she was gone, Paul scrambled to pick up the broadsides. I had tears in my eyes and Father saw them. "Be patient with your sister," he said.

"She hates me."

"She doesn't hate you. She has feelings she can't sort out. She's smitten with Amos. He hasn't finished his indenture yet. And when he does, what course is open to them? Times now are too uncertain."

For the hundredth time it came to me how my father would do anything to keep peace in his family, even while he was doing everything to make trouble with the Crown.

"Father, can I ask you a question?"

"Always."

"What matters? What's true? Or what people think?"

He put an arm around my shoulders. "You know the answer, Sarah. What matters is what's true. Always. If we didn't know that, would we thinking men here in Boston do what we're doing to defend our rights? Would they be laying plans in Philadelphia for a congress if they worried what the British think?"

Then he hugged me. It said more than words, if I knew my father. It said, "I can't make it all right. But please know I am trying."

IT WAS THE first of June. And the Port of Boston was officially closed.

Church bells rang at noon, the time of closing. Shops were shuttered up tight. People rushed to church, though it was a weekday. "God send us speedy relief," the ministers prayed.

British troops were landing at the wharves. A royal train of artillery was camped on Boston Common.

The streets were full of wagons packed with goods sent to us by other colonies. The mood was mixed. Cheer at the wagons of supplies and good wishes coming to us and somberness at the sight of the deserted wharves.

Father went to his shop that morning. He was making a copper plate for Isaiah Thomas's magazine that showed how saltpeter was made.

I'd heard him tell Rachel that if war came, America would first run out of saltpeter and gunpowder.

In our house all day, however, the mood was almost festive. Doctor Warren was coming to supper.

As I helped clean and air the house, shooed the little ones outside, and helped Rachel with the supper's fixings, things seemed as sharply etched in my sight as one of Father's engravings.

The day stands out in my mind. For a reason I still cannot fathom.

Rachel set a good table. We had cold meats and fresh fish with her special butter sauce. There were creamed vegetables, browned potatoes, a clam pie, and applesauce cake.

But I was as nervous as a cat with a long tail in a room full of rocking chairs.

Grandmother was complaining about "laying out such a feast on the board when our port is now closed and food will be scarce." And I worried that if Grandmother took the notion in her head, she would say something similar in Doctor Warren's presence. And, then, what might Debby say to embarrass me? She'd already snickered when I came downstairs wearing my good short gown and new apron.

"Act your age," she said, "before he reminds you of it."

I sighed as I set our best pewter plates on the table and prepared dishes of food for Elizabeth, Mary, and Frances, who would be fed first, then sent into the yard to play in the sweet June dusk.

How could Debby make something vile of my worshipful feelings for Doctor Warren? There were just too many things I did not understand these days.

"PROVISIONS ARE pouring in over the Neck," Doctor Warren said. He accepted a mug of cold cider, which I offered from a tray. "Rice from Charleston, South Carolina, meal and flour from Maryland, quintals of codfish from Marblehead, rye and bread from Baltimore, flour and money from Alexandria."

"Our friends in other colonies are with us," Father said.

"Yes."

They stood in front of the fireless hearth in the dining room, my brother Paul with them. Debby brought in a platter of cheese and biscuits and grapes.

"A rider came to town today with a message from Christopher Gadsden, the planter of South Carolina," my brother said. "The message was 'Don't pay for an ounce of the damned tea!' "

Paul took a huge sip of his cider. His swagger and stance were manly now that he was out of school and working with my father. No more did we run the streets at night, doing mischief after curfew. Ofttimes of an evening he worked in Father's shop or accompanied him to Benjamin Edes's newspaper office. For tonight, he had donned a clean shirt, wore a stock about his neck, and a frock coat. His shoes were polished and his breeches brushed.

Paul was deliberately placing himself apart from his sisters. It was his way of announcing that he was grown-up now. His voice was deeper, too. And he seemed at home with himself, discussing politics.

Rachel came in with a platter of fish. "Sit, gentlemen."

They sat. The air was festive. Rachel lighted candles in pewter holders on the table, and they cast a lovely glow in the half-light of the summer evening. Through the open windows came the sounds of my sisters at play in the yard.

I love candle-lighting time. All peace descends on our house, which seems to settle in with its creaking old pine floorboards and overhead beams. It's an old house, built near a hundred years ago, but it is snug and cheery.

Father said a prayer.

When it was finished, Doctor Warren looked at Grandmother. "You're looking especially gay this evening, Mother Revere."

"I'm too old for flattery, young man."

"But not for the truth. I hope we're never too old for the truth."

"Betimes the truth is too old for us." She smiled at him. "It's the new blue ribbons on my cap."

"They serve you well."

"They'll have to. They're the last new bit of frippery I'll have for a while. We're lucky if we don't starve, the lot of us, with our port now closed. Tell me, Doctor, why is it always Boston that breaks the king's peace? In New York they sent their tea ships back unharmed."

"I wouldn't worry, ma'am. I have it from a good source that Colonel Washington of the Virginia Militia told the House of Burgesses, 'If need be I will raise one thousand men and subsist them at my own expense and march, myself at their head, to the relief of Boston.' "

"Hmmph," Grandmother said. "It sounds to me like this Washington is putting himself forth to lead our army when the time comes. I say he bears watching. Those Virginians are uppity."

"It's especially good that the South is with us," Father said. He carved the cold meat and passed the plates to Rachel.

"Let's hope there will be no need for an army," Rachel put in. "My friend, Lady Frankland, says that London sent money to help us. Isn't that a hopeful sign, Doctor?"

"There are many in England who are dismayed at the closing of our port. But they aren't in Parliament," he answered.

We commenced to eat. Father paused and looked around the table, his fork midair. "Not a topsail vessel is to be seen in our harbor. Just ships of war. 'Tis a sad day for Boston."

"And troops," Paul reminded him.

"Yes, troops," Father said glumly.

"The king's own, the Forty-third and the Fifth, under Lord Percy." Paul enumerated them, feeling very important.

Across the table, I saw Debby eyeing Rachel. "How does Lady Frankland know money came from London?" she asked lightly.

"She has many friends," Rachel answered innocently, "Tory and Patriot alike."

"It must be difficult for her, keeping them from each other's throats," Debby remarked dryly.

"Not at all," Rachel said. "Everyone loves Lady Frankland. And knows her to be neutral."

"How uncommon," Debby said.

"No"—Doctor Warren fastened a cool blue gaze on my sister—"John Hancock's aunt Lydia has extended an invitation to young Lord Percy of the Fifth to dine."

"Hmmph," Grandmother growled. "I'd expect as much from Lydia Hancock. She always was a social climber."

Doctor Warren laughed. "I'm afraid she's just very taken with the young Percy's quick smile. I spoke with her this day. 'After all,' she told me, 'I'm an old lady. When will I ever again be able to look out my window and see an earl galloping across Boston Common on a grand horse?' "

"Never again, I hope," Debby mumbled.

"Confusing times for us all." And Rachel sighed.

Doctor Warren tore off a piece of his bread and explained. "Percy is in a difficult position. All he wants, at the moment, is to be a pleasant guest in a rebellious town. And make a good impression on the Hancocks. Like General Gage, he likes Americans. But make no mistake about it. Nice as they are, we're plotting against them. And if they can prove it, they'll hang us, every one. Ship us to England first and do it proper-like."

It got quiet as second helpings were passed around. I saw my sister Frances listening outside the window.

Then Rachel spoke. "Doctor Warren, speaking of General Gage, I would ask you a favor."

I thought Debby would drop her fork.

"Anything, dear lady," Warren said.

"As you know, Margaret Gage, wife of the general, is American."

"Ah, yes. A beautiful heiress. Of the Kemble family from New Jersey, I believe."

"I've never met her, but she is a good friend of Lady Frankland's. I've been told by Agnes that Margaret has severe headaches. And now that the Gages find themselves in Boston, she would seek a doctor."

Warren helped himself to more fish. "There are doctors aplenty in Boston. All good ones. Church, Young, Kast, Danforth, and Jeffries." He smiled. "Jeffries might be more suited to her. He's a Tory. Though he swears like a drunken parrot."

"Mrs. Gage is very fastidious," Rachel said. "And you have a reputation for being clean. Something most doctors pay scant attention to."

I saw Debby's lip curl in disdain.

"Would you see her?" Rachel asked. "Lady Frankland begged me to ask."

Warren nodded, thinking. "The wife of

Gage," he mused. "I can scarce refuse. Yet, what would her husband think if she came to me?"

"That she seeks the best doctor in town," Rachel said.

Debby kicked me under the table.

Warren gave the matter thought, then met Rachel's eyes. The moment was heavy with meaning. I saw my father smiling serenely at Rachel.

What matters? What people think? Or what's true?

"What brings on her headaches?" Warren asked.

"Lady Frankland believes Mrs. Gage is sore afflicted by the trouble between England and America," Rachel said.

"Aren't we all?" Debby put in snidely.

They paid her no mind. "I had heard the woman's loyalties were divided," Warren said. His eyes grew bluer now.

"Mrs. Gage will be most discreet," Rachel promised.

Warren nodded. He seemed to understand something that eluded the rest of us. "Very well. Tell Lady Frankland I will see Mrs. Gage." Then to Father, "This is as good a meal as I've had in a fortnight, Paul. Though my man, Damien, is a good cook."

"You must get yourself a wife, Joseph."

"I fear the best one in Boston has been taken."

My head swam. I could think only of Debby's accusations against them. I got up to help clear the dishes and bring in the dessert. The conversation took another turn.

But it seemed as if the light outside had changed somehow. As if there had been an eclipse. Or some benighted form had moved across the sun. Did not anyone else notice it? I turned around. They had not. The chatter at the table was as lively as ever.

In the kitchen, Debby caught my eye. There was a sneer on her face. I felt sick. Did she really think there was something unsavory between Doctor Warren and Rachel?

What matters? What's true? Or what people think? What's true, Father had said. But was he blind? He had heard what had just transpired, seen it, but only smiled at Rachel. With love and pride in his eyes.

Oh God, I prayed, *help me to know what matters. And what's true. And don't let Debby be right.*

After supper that night, Doctor Warren took us children outside. In the gathering June twilight, he told us what I already knew.

"Your stepmother is to have a baby. You must be especially considerate of her. And be helpful to her in small ways. And not quarrel or be in a bad temper."

"Will the baby die?" Mary asked.

"No," Doctor Warren said, "your stepmother is healthy. There is no reason to believe the baby will not be, too."

"Will it wet the bed?" Elizabeth asked.

"I am sure it will. For a while," he said gravely.

"Will it be a boy?" came from Frances.

"Mayhap it will be. Would you like a brother?"

"I'd like to be a boy," Frances said. Though she had stopped dressing in boy's clothing, she still slept in her shoes. We could not break her of this.

"Well, you aren't a boy," Doctor Warren told her. "But you are a very lovely little girl. And you should take your shoes off when you go to bed."

"I told everyone they would come," Frances said gravely. "Now they are here. So tonight I'm leaving on my clothes when I go to bed."

"Who?" Doctor Warren asked.

"The British. They have come to get us. Because we were naughty, what we did with the tea. I heard you say that if they can prove we're plotting, they'll hang us, every one."

Doctor Warren knelt down and peered into her face. "Frances, the British are not going to hurt you. Or anyone in your family. They don't hurt the families of men who plot against them."

"Will they hang my father?"

"No. I promise you. I am president of the Boston Committee of Safety. And I will not permit it."

My sister's gray eyes went wide.

"It is my job," Warren went on, "to get anyone the British plan to harm out of Boston. And I will get your father out if I hear they plan to harm him."

"All right," she said. "Then I'll not sleep in my clothes. But I'll keep my shoes on, if it's all the same to you."

Warren hugged her, then stood up. "Debby? Paul? Sarah? If your father must leave again and there are any more such problems, let me know. Don't bother Rachel."

We promised we would and he went into the house. Frances hugged me and I held her close. Nobody said anything. Doctor Warren had used the spell of the June night and the tenderness of the moment to bind us together, as clearly as if he had bound us with a lint bandage. And right then not even Debby had the desire to undo what he had done.

The man could work magic. But then, he was a physician. It was his job to get people to trust him. I only wished I could go on doing so. That I could stay caught in the spell he had cast on us, forever.

Chapter Eight

*S*IX MONTHS LATER, in December of 1774, I sat in my parents' room, holding the new baby. His name was Joshua.

My father had had a second son and was very pleased.

Sleet and snow made a pattering sound on the windows. A fire in the hearth roared.

Five days ago Rachel had been brought to childbed. This morning the house had been full of people paying their respects. As was the custom they came right into my parents' room, where Rachel was propped up in her best cotton-

and-lace nightdress and cap to receive them. Wine and cake were served. Gifts were left.

Now Rachel lay napping. The baby slept in his cradle. I sat reading *Tom Jones*. The house was very quiet. Debby had taken the children to market, not that much was to be had at market these days. But the selectmen gave out food. Yet it was not charity. Every man worked for his family's share. The town fathers had started projects. Streets and wharves were repaired, docks cleaned.

My father, of course, had his work. He rode at the behest of the Whigs.

He had been to New York in the middle of the summer, to New York and Philadelphia early in September, and Philadelphia late in September. In October he had gone to Philadelphia again.

And now he was leaving for Portsmouth, New Hampshire. In the sleet and the rain. It was only a one-day trip, but that was not the point.

The point was, it was only five days since his wife had given birth. Rachel hid her disappointment well. Father was now at Doctor Warren's house on Hanover Street conferring.

I sat wondering what Debby would bring home from market. Doctor Warren had said that Rachel was healthy but that she needed a special diet.

Warren had not delivered the baby. A midwife had done that. But he had come to pay her an official call.

"Good food," he told Father. "Good milk and cheese and meat. And she will be up and about scolding you in no time."

Of course, Doctor Warren jested. But Father frowned. I knew what he was thinking. I'd heard him tell his mother. "Not a good time to have a babe," he'd said.

And to Warren, he'd suggested, "Perhaps I can bring some supplies back from Portsmouth."

"Good thinking," Doctor Warren said.

My mind strayed from my book. I heard voices downstairs, raised in greeting. We had another visitor. I felt exasperated. Rachel needed no more visitors this day. She needed peace. I got up to close the door, then instead went down a few steps and peered over the banister.

Our visitor was Lady Frankland.

"She's asleep," I heard Grandmother say. I also heard the distaste in her voice.

"Then I'll leave my gift and the basket."

"We need no Tory food," Grandmother told her.

I dropped my book and ran down the stairs. "Lady Frankland! How nice of you to come. Rachel will be so happy to see you!"

"She's had her share of visitors this day," Grandmother objected.

"I'm sorry I couldn't get here sooner." Lady Frankland handed her cloak to me and took the chair I drew forth in the parlor. "But Margaret had one of her headaches again this morning. She was staying with me a few days, you know, and I felt responsible. So I brought her to Doctor Warren's early this day, then back to my house. She's resting. So I took this opportunity to come."

"I'm so glad you did," I said. "Rachel is sleeping now, but I can wake her. The sight of you will do her good."

"You will *not* wake her!" Grandmother said. "She needs her strength and rest."

I faced my grandmother. "A visit from her friend will give her strength," I said. I faced her down. She turned away, mumbling.

"Come upstairs with me, Lady Frankland." I

picked up her basket. It was very heavy. In her hand she had something else, wrapped in oiled paper.

She followed me with a rustling of silk skirts. I could smell her perfume. It was heavenly.

"The food in the basket is not from me," she whispered. "It's from Margaret Gage."

"Mrs. Gage sent food?"

"Yes. Butter, fresh ham, biscuits, cheese, dried fruit."

Fancy that! Food for Rachel from the wife of the British commander-in-chief. Though I'd wager he didn't know of it. "But why?"

"She is ever so grateful that your stepmother made the connection with her and Doctor Warren. He helps her headaches."

I must remember. Margaret Kemble Gage was an American after all. "I see. But you said she was staying with you."

"She frequently does. Don't tell anyone, but she and the general aren't getting on. He says she is difficult, that she lectures him about liberty and justice. So she has frequent sojourns away from him."

"Oh."

"This gift I have in hand is a christening dress.

I embroidered it myself. When will the babe be christened? In spring?"

"No, next Sunday." I almost said, "After my father returns from Portsmouth," but checked myself.

"In this weather?"

We were on the landing. I turned to her and smiled. "My father was carried to the Cockerel on the first day of January, in rain and sleet just like this for christening."

She put a hand on my arm. She was no longer a young woman, but she wore her wrinkles like a soldier wears epaulets. "I am so glad you voiced your objections over Mother Revere to let me see my friend," she said.

And we went into the room to see Rachel.

GENERAL GAGE had 3,000 soldiers in town. North Square itself was filled with Royal Marines, who were billeted in every house with a spare room. Father had Paul walk me and the little ones to school every day and fetch us home in the afternoon.

The Royal Irish and the Forty-third were on Back Street, not far from us. Major Pitcairn himself was at our neighbors's, the Shaws.

The Shaws were near violent in their anti-British sentiments. And they had two young sons, fifteen and fourteen. I was with Father when he hailed Josiah and Michael on the street one day and asked them how they were bearing up.

"It's not Pitcairn himself," Josiah told my father, "it's that damned Lieutenant Wragg. He puts down the Americans at every turn."

"Major Pitcairn tries to keep the peace," Michael said.

"He's a tough old soldier," Father said, "but he is honest and true. He makes a point of getting on with men who do not share his political views. So bide your tongues. And your time. If you get too nettled, come to my shop and talk to me."

You would think, what with the Sixty-fourth on Castle Island and the marines on top of all of us, Gage would be happy. But he was not.

"He's afraid," my brother Paul told me as he was walking us home from school one day. The little girls walked a distance ahead. "He's afraid because he knows that the people of this province can muster ten times that many in a day to march against him."

Since September first, when Gage had sent men to remove the largest supply of gunpowder in our province from the Provincial Powder House six miles north of Boston, the people had been angry.

The next day thousands marched on Cambridge Common and "visited" the houses of leading Tories and put them out of their homes.

The people had shown their strength. They had assembled from various towns in fifteen minutes. They had sent riders with the alarm to other towns.

They had amassed together, fully equipped for action.

And General Gage grew sore afraid. The farmers, artisans, and mechanics of Massachusetts were not the country bumpkins he took them for.

My brother Paul knew little. Father made certain none of us knew what was really going on.

We did know that Gage had heavy cannon on Roxbury Neck, because he feared that "the country people might storm the town."

We did know that after that September "powder alarm," my father and his Whig friends had formed themselves into committees to watch the movements of the British soldiers.

And that is how they learned that now, in the middle of winter, British warships on our coast were likely heading for Portsmouth to strengthen Fort William and Mary. Because only six British soldiers guarded the place. And the Americans might attack. One of those warships was a ship of the line, HMS *Somerset*.

Father was to warn the people of Portsmouth that a British expedition was coming.

So once again my brother Paul held a prancing and game Militia's reins in the yard. Paul had given the mare an extra supply of oats and a special rubdown. She was restless, anxious to be on her way. You would swear she knew, all of a piece, that horse, what she was about.

Once again, Father put on his spurs. We stood around him and watched.

"Care for the little ones," he told me and Debby.

"Yes, Father." I gave him one of his saddle-bags. "You've bread and meat and some cheese."

He nodded. "No one goes out after dark. And when you walk to school, Sarah, you and Paul, cast an eye. And attract no unnecessary attention."

I promised.

"Amos says you'll never get out of town without a pass from Gage," Debby said.

"I intend to get one. I'm on my way to Province House now."

"What reason will you give?" she asked.

"Reason?" Father shrugged and smiled. "I'm a silversmith. On my way to sell silver. What other reason?"

It was the first time he needed a pass to get out of town. But if he was worried, he didn't show it. "Don't have a care," he said to us. "I'll be at the house of Samuel Cutts in Portsmouth tomorrow this time. It's only sixty miles."

It had snowed on the ninth. It was now the twelfth, and the snow rutted the ground, froze, and drifted in the freezing wind.

"Now, kisses, my lambs."

We kissed him, each in turn. He had said farewell to Rachel in their room, where she was still abed.

"Mother?" He put his arm around her. "Take care of my brood."

"Go off with ye," she said, and pushed him away. But I saw tears in her eyes as she turned. Was it dangerous, then? Did he becalm us with false cheer?

He went outside and took Militia's reins from Paul, who came in and secured the door with special care.

I peered outside, watching him go. He walked Militia at a leisurely pace, not wishing to attract attention. I saw a British officer at the corner wave to him. Father waved back. He always returned decency in kind to the British soldiers. And Tories.

"I respond to the man," he told us, "not to his politics."

His head was bent in the wind. It was late morning, yet the day took on the cast of dusk. A swirling storm was coming, so we had not gone to school today.

I sighed and turned. We older ones would be hard put to keep the little ones entertained.

BECAUSE OF my father's message, four hundred militiamen mustered in Portsmouth, collected boats, and assaulted the fort before the British got there.

They took possession, hauled down the king's colors, and made off with a hundred barrels of gunpowder.

By the time Father returned the night of the second day, he was a marked man. Gage knew he had carried the news. Soldiers on the street were talking of it. One of them had yelled out to Paul, "Tell your father he's fortunate we have such a lenient commander."

My father did not act like a marked man.

He hailed the same British soldiers on the street in greeting, as he walked Militia by them. He shouted for his family, who came running.

He was in great spirits. He brought a side of mutton, a bag of flour, slabs of cheese, and a bottle of Madeira.

"From the Portsmouth Whigs," he told us, "in honor of little Joshua. Where is he? Where is my new son?"

Rachel came down the steps, the babe in her arms. I stood beside her. She wore a new shawl Lady Frankland had sent.

It was her first trip below stairs since she gave birth.

"You're home," she said as she always did. "No rope around your neck?" Rachel had a macabre sense of humor, betimes. And I minded that this time it was not all humor.

"No rope, my girl."

"Paul," she said, standing there with little Joshua in her arms, "Gage knows all about you. His soldiers bandy your name about on the streets."

Father smiled. "I just said hello to one on the street. He inquired after our new son."

"Paul, will you never stop believing in the goodness of human nature?" she asked.

He shrugged and held out his arms. "How can I, my dear? When you convince me of it anew, every day?"

She went to him.

We ate in the kitchen that night, near the fire, talking and passing Joshua around. Wind howled outside, but we were well fed and cosy.

Then came the unmistakable sound of tramping footsteps. We fell silent, looking at one another.

Father smiled. "Gage will not arrest me," he said. "He has great respect for the rule of law. Now, did I tell you how some New Hampshire men marched over frozen ground to the fort?

And others paddled down the Piscataqua River amid swirling snow?"

We listened, taking heart from his cheer, his confidence, his reassurance.

Father was not arrested. But it was the last time he was able to get a pass from the British to get out of Boston. The British watched him closely now. He kept a small boat hidden somewhere on the banks of the river in the North End.

He told nobody where. Not even us.

Chapter Nine

*F*ATHER TURNED FORTY in December. Debby made him a honey raisin cake. I presented him with a new shirt I'd sewn. Rachel had knitted a muffler, cap, and hose.

Paul gave him a new ledger in which to keep customers' orders and to sketch. My father liked to first draw things he planned to make: sugar tongs, spoons, a Freemason medal.

Doctor Warren came with a bottle of Madeira. He was wearing pistols.

Father raised his eyebrows. "Have things come to such a turn?"

The small children were out of earshot. Warren spoke softly. "I was visiting a patient, near the gallows on the Neck. Three British officers hailed me. One said, 'You'll soon come to the gallows, Warren.'"

"They're bored and restless," Father said. "Careful, Joseph, we can't let it get like last time."

Warren nodded. His face was pale. He looked across the hall to the parlor where Rachel sat nursing Joshua.

I saw him stare at her as if he had never seen her before. And not as a doctor, but as a man looks at a woman.

Rachel looked up and smiled. Yes, she had a shawl around her, but it did not completely conceal her nakedness. Did she have no shame? Or did she see him as a doctor? And not as a friend?

I did not know. I was beset with confusion. And I did not know how to take Doctor Warren, or anything he said, after that incident. I no longer knew how to regard him.

IT WAS a terrible long winter. All I recollect is snow and sleet, having constantly to sand the floors for the mud tracked in, the smell of damp clothes on the rope strung in the kitchen to dry at night, the younger children sniffling and having raspy throats. Someone was always coughing in the house, and the sound of it mingled with the musket fire of the British infantry shooting at floating targets in the harbor.

We missed a lot of school for the weather. Father wouldn't let us go. The Royal Irish Regiment had malignant spotted fever. It was rumored that Gage's own confidential secretary had died from the throat distemper.

Father feared sickness more than anything. He feared for his "lambs," he said. So he kept us from school often. Which left us in the house, ofttimes at each other's throats.

The visits of Doctor Warren and Lady Frankland were the only bright spots for Rachel and the children. Lady Frankland came at least once a week. She'd bring seed cakes for the children. Or a pretty book. She started Frances doing a sampler and even rolled up her sleeves and donned an apron one day to engage us in making apple tarts.

Then she and Rachel would sit in the parlor with baby Joshua and have coffee and talk.

I don't know if Grandmother disapproved more of her's or Doctor Warren's visits. "That man is here again," she'd say. She'd taken to calling him "that man" instead of Doctor.

Warren's horse was often tied at our hitching post. He came on any pretense, it seemed—to dine, to bring baskets of food for Rachel, to check on the baby or my little sisters, to plot with my father.

He came when Father rode away to visit the New Hampshire Congress in Exeter in January.

We arrived home from school with Paul one afternoon to find him there. Grandmother was out. He sat at the kitchen table. Rachel was making bread dough. He sat drinking coffee and watching her. The children ran to him as we came into the house and he took them on his lap, one at a time.

I decided to ask my brother what he thought of it. I followed him to the yard when he went for wood.

"What do you suppose they find to talk about?" I asked.

"Who?"

"Doctor Warren and Rachel."

He was gathering kindling in his arms. "Why do you ask?"

"Well, don't you ever wonder?"

"I've too many other things to wonder about. Like how the British Regulars are bored, angry, and haven't enough to eat."

"What has that to do with us?"

"Plenty. The other day some of them attacked the town watch. Many are deserting. Gage could retaliate."

"Oh, you men, is war all you think of?"

He stood with kindling piled high in his arms. "Hold out your apron."

I did so.

He dropped some kindling in it and went for more. "And what do you women think of? Don't get like Debby, Sarah."

"And how is that?"

"Suspicious of Rachel."

"I'm not. I don't want to be."

"Rachel and Warren have much to discuss. Father doesn't worry it. Why should you? Or are you jealous?"

"Of what?"

He grinned at me as we walked toward the house. "That he pays her more mind than you."

I blushed and did not even give him the courtesy of a reply. I would not do him the honor. Besides, I did not have one.

THAT NIGHT, as I lay abed unable to sleep, I heard a sound downstairs. Was Father home? Voices, low and muted, came to me. Had I been sleeping? Was I dreaming?

The house was chilled, but I roused myself out of bed, threw a blanket around my shoulders, and crept quietly out into the hall without waking Debby.

Voices, to be sure. In the kitchen. I eased myself down the stairs and stood in the darkened hallway, shivering.

The kitchen was cast with an eerie light. In it I saw Rachel. In her nightclothes.

Two men were with her. One form was tall and thin. I would recognize it anywhere. Doctor Warren!

The other was thin, too, and bent over. He had a strange voice and he huddled close to the fire.

"Here's some sterling." Doctor Warren handed the man some money. "Rachel? Do you have food?"

"Right here."

The man put the food in his haversack.

"A boat awaits at the riverbank at the foot of Clark's Wharf," Doctor Warren said. "It will take you to the town of Andover. You will be met there and taken to a safe house."

I suddenly realized why the man's voice was strange. He was British! And it came to me then. He was a British soldier. He was deserting. And Rachel and Doctor Warren were helping him!

I closed my eyes and minded what I'd heard in the streets. And what my brother had said. That many British soldiers were deserting. They were being spirited by boat across the Charles, aided by townspeople.

I leaned against the wainscoting. My breath came in spurts. In the kitchen there was movement. And I was aware that the man was being escorted out the side door by Doctor Warren.

I saw Rachel secure it, then turn and come into the hallway. Quietly, I pattered up the stairs, shivering, and went to bed.

WHO KNEW? Was Father in on it? Next morning he was at the breakfast table—lingering, smiling, cuddling Joshua, playing with the children—

while Rachel put the ingredients for stew in a pot over the hearth and Grandmother dozed in the corner over her second cup of tea.

Did my brother Paul know?

Of a sudden it came to me that we were all locked away from each other in our house.

Half the time I suspected Paul of seditious activities. I'd changed my mind about my brother. I decided he knew too much. That very morning at breakfast he told Father that Doctor Church, a staunch Whig, was "keeping company with Captain Price, a British officer."

Father listened politely, all the while smiling. He did entirely too much smiling these days for my liking.

"My friend is an apprentice for Church," Paul said. "He says Church dines frequently with Price and Robinson, a commissioner."

Father was attentive.

"My friend says Church usually has little or no money," Paul went on, anxious to show Father what he had learned, "but lately Church has had several hundred brand new British guineas."

Father thanked Paul and told him to keep it

quiet. Father, of course, did not tell us half of what he was about. Now I wondered. Was Paul spying for him?

And what of Lady Frankland? She swept into the house bringing sweetmeats and charming the children. But what was she really here for?

Debby's whole purpose in life was to see Amos. Since our house was always being watched, it had been decided that for his own safety he should not come around anymore. So she sneaked out to see him. Lord knew what they did when they met.

Doctor Warren came in the middle of the night to help Rachel give aid to a deserter. And when he wasn't doing that he was talking in low tones with Rachel in corners. Or eyeing her like a smitten schoolboy.

Grandmother trusted no one, but mumbled disagreeably and fostered distrust.

All I wanted was for my family to be of one piece, to *be* a family again. For a while it had been good. But now it was coming apart, unraveling like an old coat before my eyes.

What mattered? What was true? Or what I thought? I did not know. But I don't ever remember being so frightened.

Chapter Ten

I SUPPOSE IF PUSHED I would have to admit that as a child I had always loved Doctor Warren, the same as Mary, Frances, and Elizabeth loved him now. Like they did, I would climb on his lap for the maple sugar he brought out of his deep pockets.

When I was a little girl, I called him "Uncle Doctor." Now I just said Doctor. I was a child no longer and painfully mindful of the stirrings I felt when in his presence. Ofttimes they confused and shamed me. At the same time I felt insufficient in the presence of his impeccable person.

The sight of the snow-white ruffles at his neck

and wrists and the stringent but fragrant smell of the soap he used pleasured me.

Always I wished I was more attractive, like Debby. And could behave as she did toward him. She was saucy with him. She sassed him prettily. He accepted it in good cheer.

I would sit quietly in a corner when my sisters clambered over him and listen to his stories. One story was of the great smallpox epidemic of '64. It was he who had been called in when the dreaded disease came to our house.

He treated me as well as Debby and Paul. I have no recollection of it. I'd been only two. But he stood by my father when Father went to the selectmen and begged that we not be sent to the pesthouse.

Warren was now thirty-four, just six years younger than Father. But I thought of him as years younger. He appeared boyish to me, though I knew he'd been a doctor since he was twenty, when he graduated Harvard and served under Doctor Lloyd.

Yes, I had always loved him, as a benevolent friend or uncle. The fact that my feelings toward him had changed of late, I had tried to keep well hidden. I knew his had not changed toward me.

He would smile at me—sitting there in Father's chair while my sisters climbed over him—and say something about my handwork, to make me feel grown-up. Occasionally, he still tugged my hair or teased me. I blushed violently when he did this.

Now, suddenly, everything was different. Now I knew that I must say something to him about Rachel.

Father wore blinders where Rachel was concerned. He had always been able to spirit himself up for causes. But the everyday problems in his life he preferred to ignore, thinking they would go away.

There was no hope for Debby or Paul doing it. So as much as I loved and admired Warren, the desire to keep my family all of a piece was stronger than anything.

I HAD my chance sooner than I expected.

On a Friday in February, my brother was given a message on the street by someone he trusted, one of those faceless stable boys who overheard British officers talking while he worked at caring for their horses.

"Word has it that the Sixty-fourth, on Castle

Island, is setting off for Salem to collect materials of war that would be used for armed insurrection," I heard him tell Father.

On Saturday Debby and I had just delivered Father's noon meal to his shop. Paul was not there. Father drew me aside.

"I don't want your sister to know, or she'll tell Amos and he'll want to come along. But this afternoon, I and two other men are rowing over to Castle Island to see what's acting with the Sixty-fourth. Paul is bringing my boat to the point of embarkation. Give this note to Rachel."

I took the note.

"Deliver it only to Rachel. I'll be back this evening."

Before I gave Rachel the note, I read it. I know it was wrong, but I didn't care. The note said they were embarking from the banks by Clark's Wharf and would return there this evening.

He never came.

By dusk, which still came early, Rachel was convinced that something had happened to him.

"He's been taken." She was wringing her hands. "Paul? Go find Doctor Warren. Ask him to come."

Always Doctor Warren, I thought bitterly. I was angry. And afraid.

My brother went out into the dampness of the early evening. Rachel told us to sit and eat. "Where is Debby?"

"With Amos," I said.

"Why isn't she here? I told her to be in before dark."

I reached for my cloak. "I'll go fetch her."

"No," Rachel said. "I don't need you running the streets, too. Besides, you don't look well."

I had a headache. My "woman's time" was coming on. "I'm all right," I said. "I know where they are. I can be back in half an hour."

She agreed reluctantly. "Take Ruffles with you."

So I took a lantern and the dog. Ruffles was small and scruffy but protective. He'd just as soon snap at a British sentry as a street rat. And he trudged faithfully beside me on the wet cobblestones down Fish Street.

British soldiers were shadowy figures in the fog that came in off the water. They nodded or took off their tricorn hats in greeting. I had my basket over my arm, so I looked like a young woman with a mission.

I did not go to fetch Debby. I could not care a copper where Debby was. I was going to the banks under Clark's Wharf. To try to sight my father.

HE DID not come.

I stood alone with Ruffles near the pilings under the wharf, holding my single lantern in the freezing mist. I was determined to wait for Father that night and bring him home to Rachel.

But he did not come.

Someone else did. After about an hour, when I was snuggled against a wood piling on some empty crates, shivering and frightened at every turn, with Ruffles in my arms, the dog began to growl.

I looked up to see a tall figure approaching. "Sarah?"

It was Doctor Warren. He came walking down the embankment, his lantern light spilling ahead of him. "Sarah Revere? Is that you, child?"

"No, it is not Sarah Revere, the child," I said. "It is Sarah Revere, the young woman."

He set his lantern down. "Forgive me that I did not recognize her sooner." His familiar voice was rich with amusement.

Silence, except for the lapping of the water.

"What are you doing here, Sarah?"

"Waiting for my father."

"How do you know where he'll come in?"

"I know this place. He used to keep his boat here before he found it necessary to hide it. And the note gave the exact location."

"Ah, you read the note."

"Yes."

"Well, Rachel thought you did. She sent me looking for you. She's frantic with worry."

"Tell her I'm all right."

"Come along and tell her yourself."

"I've a mind to wait."

"He's not coming, Sarah." The words were said with sadness.

In the light of the lanterns I looked up into the familiar comfort of his handsome, kind face. "What's happened?"

"Word came to me. The British were waiting for them in the shoals off Castle Island. We think it was a trap to put him under lock and key while the Sixty-fourth streamed out of the harbor on a transport to Cape Ann."

"They've *taken* him?"

"Yes." He smiled. "Don't worry. They'll let

him go. They just want him to cool his heels a little."

Tears came to my eyes. "So he's in prison! Does Rachel know?"

"Yes. But he'll be home. Likely they'll release him after the weekend. They don't want him bringing any warnings to Marblehead or Salem. Don't say anything to your brother. He's devastated that the message he brought led to this."

In prison. My father. I snatched up the lantern and began to walk off. "Well, I hope you're happy now," I said.

"Sarah?" I heard his voice behind me, low, puzzled. "What is it, child? He'll be all right. What do you mean? Why should I be happy?"

I turned, halfway up the embankment. In the last hour the wind had picked up. The mist had blown off. There was a half-moon. But it gave good enough light so that I could see his tall figure outlined against the silvery water. "Because," I said, "now you can keep Rachel company all weekend. It's what you want, isn't it?"

And I ran home, Ruffles at my heels.

THE WORDS shame me. To this day. But at the moment they gave vent to my feelings. Letting them out was like opening a floodgate behind which the waters of my anger boiled.

I went home and into the house and threw off my cloak. I ran past Grandmother, Debby, and the children, ignoring their startled faces.

"It's Church," Paul was saying to Rachel. He stood hunched, miserably, hands thrust into his breeches. "I know it is! The British are sensible of every movement the Whigs make! Someone is telling them. I know it's Doctor Church."

"You'll never get your father or the others to believe that," Rachel said.

I ran by them, upstairs to my room, kicked off my shoes, and got into bed. Under my muffler, I wished I could be like Frances and keep my shoes on.

I knew now why she did it. It was in part an act of rebellion and in part a manner of being prepared. Lying there fully dressed, I felt as if I could get up and run out any time I chose. No one could catch me unawares and put me at a disadvantage.

I was wrong. There are different ways to catch one unawares and put one at a disadvantage.

A knock came on the door. I did not answer.

"Sarah?"

It was him! Come to beset me more. Why couldn't he go away?

The door opened and he came in. The room was dark, but he carried a single candle. He set it down and drew up a chair.

"I think we should talk, Sarah."

"Go away."

"I'm not going to oblige you, so you may as well turn your head and look at me."

I lay still. My head hurt and I was shivering, whether from the piercing cold I'd stood in for over an hour or from anger, I did not know. It did not matter.

"Sarah, this thing is between us now. And it will fester and give us both a mortification of the spirit. It must be purged."

Still, I did not answer.

"Good Lord, I don't know whether to administer to you tonight or to your brother. He's downstairs blaming himself because he brought this message and it proved a trap. He needs me as much as you do."

"Go to him, then."

"Sarah, we've known each other a long time. I hold you in high esteem. I would hope you feel about me in kind."

Something wrenched inside me where I supposed my heart was. A cry strangled in my throat.

"Sarah?" I felt a hand on my head. Then, "You're feverish, child."

I sat up. The sudden motion made my head throb. "I'm not a child! When will you come to understand? Now leave me be!"

I spoke so sharply, he withdrew his hand, gave me a puzzled look, picked up his candle, and went out of the room.

I lay back down. There was a raspy feeling in my throat. I was probably coming down with some vile sickness. I thought of Father behind bars in a dank cell on Castle Island. The thought made my heart want to burst.

I heard Grandmother in the hallway ushering the children to bed. She scolded Frances to take off her shoes. It was the usual bedtime argument. Frances always won.

"You need a good whipping," Grandmother growled, going past my door.

Frances shouted something back. *Good for you,* I thought, *don't give up your shoes. Don't let them ever catch you unawares.*

Then the house quieted. I must have dozed.

I was dreaming I was a child again, climbing on Doctor Warren's lap. I could smell the scent of the soap he used, the crisp cleanness of his shirt.

"Sarah?"

I wasn't dreaming. He was bending over me.

"I've some medicine here I want you to take. Sit up."

My eyelids did not want to open. I felt as if someone had put flatirons on them. My head pounded and everything hurt. I was shivering and dying. And I was determined not to let him help me.

"Sit up and drink this."

"No."

"Come on now, Sarah."

There was no point to it. I couldn't sit up. "I can't."

"Yes, you can. Come now, Sarah."

The voice harkened back in my mind, echoed through the years. And I sat up.

The candle cast long shadows. Moonlight shone in the window. Cool hands on my head, on my forehead, on my face, my neck—professional, impersonal, yet healing.

"Thirsty," I said.

"Good. Drink."

I drank. It was tea, hot, with herbs. I pushed it away. "I don't drink tea."

"It's your grandmother's."

"All the more reason."

"Sarah, you know that the staunchest Patriot believes the sick are allowed to drink tea."

"I'm not sick."

"That is a matter for conjecture." The voice was filled with bitter irony. And brooked no argument. "Drink." He held out the cup. "As your doctor, I order it."

I drank. The hot liquid soothed my throat.

"What's in it should cure what ails you by morning. Except for your foul temper. I've no remedy for that."

"I have reason."

"We'll not discuss it now."

"I'll discuss it whenever I choose." I glared at him.

He sighed. "Very well. Then let's clear the air. Shall we?"

"Yes."

"I have no designs on your stepmother, Sarah. Your father is my dearest friend. I tell you now that I have never touched Rachel, never said a single improper thing to her. I would die before I betrayed your father in such a way. How could you ever think such a thing?"

My head had cleared of sleep. I fixed my eyes on him. "I'm not the only one in this house who thinks it."

"I am not interested in the opinion of others. Nor should you be."

What matters? What people think? Or what's true?

"I am interested in what *you* think, however. And what you have said greatly disturbs me."

"If it isn't true, why should it?"

"You have a sharp tongue in your head, my girl. I'll put it down to the fever."

"Put it down to common sense."

He looked so solemn and sad. "I would like my daughter to grow up like you. But if you were my daughter, I'm afraid I'd have to shake you until your teeth rattled at this moment."

The idea that he saw me like a daughter shook me to my bones. And made me want to cry. It was so cutting, so diminishing. And then I thought, *why, he wants me to feel this way! It's his way of getting back at me.*

"Are you sure," he asked, "that you are not

fashioning things in your mind because you're a bit jealous of Rachel?"

"Jealous?"

"Yes. She is a fine, good woman. She is pretty, she is smart, she can hold her own. Your father is a fortunate man."

"I thought you had no designs on her."

"I am a man, Sarah. Not without honor, but not made of stone, either. The Lord did not intend us to be so."

I took his meaning then and hated him for it. He found Rachel attractive, in spite of all his talk of honor. And again, he was punishing me by letting me know it.

"Do you think you are so handsome to women that they are all smitten with you?" I asked.

He thought for a moment. "A question for a question, Sarah. You consider yourself a woman now, I take it?"

"Yes. If you don't, it's no fault of mine."

He nodded. "Then my advice to you is to act like one. Now I must go downstairs and talk to Paul. He needs me, too."

And with that he picked up his candle and started to leave the room. Then something caught his eye and he stopped.

He picked up a small book on a nearby table. *"The Sonnets of William Shakespeare,"* he said. "Is this yours?"

"Why else would it be there? Do you think I'm not capable of reading it?" I was starting to sound like Grandmother.

He looked at me sadly. "I've always loved this book. I lost my only copy." Then, holding it closed in his hand, he recited:

"No longer mourn for me when I am dead, than you shall hear the surly sullen bell, give warning to the world that I am fled, from this vile world, with vilest worms to dwell. Nay, if you read this line, remember not, the hand that writ it, for I love you so, that I in your sweet thoughts would be forgot, if thinking on me then should make you woe."

The sound of his voice mesmerized me. I had no words left. He put the book down and left the room.

Chapter Eleven

*T*HE REASON FATHER was so amiable with the British soldiers who walked our streets was because, in his words, "we mustn't let it get like last time."

He meant the last time British troops were in Boston, in 1770. That time, trouble between them and the colonists had led to what Father and the other Whigs now called the Boston Massacre.

Every year, on the fifth of March, they kept the anniversary of that massacre. Once again this year, they were holding that celebration in Old South Meeting. John Hancock had been the speaker last year.

This year it was Doctor Warren. And the elder members of my family were all going. I was not.

I SAT WATCHING Debby set a new mobcap on her head, primping in front of the one mirror in our room, pinching her cheeks for color, pulling down her stays to display just the right amount of bosom. Amos was fetching her and escorting her to the affair.

"You don't have to stay home and watch the little ones, you know. Rachel said she'd take them along. They go to church of a Sunday. This is no different."

"I don't mind."

She cast me a sidelong glance. The cap was off again and she ran a hand through her shining dark curls. "Don't you think I look better without it?"

"Yes, but you know it isn't seemly to go without one."

She sighed. "You fought with him, didn't you?"

"Who?"

"Don't pretend with me. Doctor Warren. You haven't spoken to him in weeks. You're giving him an uneven time of it. Everyone notices."

"It's my affair if I did."

"You were outright rude to him when he was here last Sunday."

"Last Sunday all he and Father did was talk of how he knocked that British sentry down with his fist, right out on the street."

"He *is* brave, isn't he?"

"Stupid is more the word for it."

"Well, the sentry did challenge him. And all he was doing was coming home from visiting a patient."

"Since when are you taking up for him? I thought you hated him. All you've done is spirit me up to think he's carrying on with Rachel."

She turned from the mirror to look at me. "I only voiced my fears. You shouldn't let people tell you what to think. I did it to show you he's just a man, with weaknesses like any other. You were so smitten with him."

"I'm not smitten with him, Debby."

"I'd like to know what you call it, then."

"I always held him in great esteem. After all, he did save us all from smallpox."

She went back to the mirror and fluffed the ruffle of the chemise out from under the stays at the neckline. "He didn't save me," she said.

I stared at her. "You're alive, aren't you?"

"Sometimes I wish I weren't."

"Debby! What a thing to say! Why, it's a sin against everything we've been taught!"

Her beautiful blue eyes filled with tears. She turned to me. "Look at me. What do you see?"

"You're beautiful, Debby. Everyone says so. You're the prettier one and you always have been."

"Look again."

"You mean the scars?"

"Yes. How do you think I feel every time I look into a mirror?"

"People don't pay mind to them," I said. "Not when they really know you."

"I do. Not a day in my life goes by that I don't pay mind to them."

"You blame Doctor Warren for them?"

"Why do you think you don't have any scars?"

"Grandmother says I had a favorably light dose."

"Grandmother lies. He inoculated you. You had a light dose *because* of the inoculation. You and Paul. He didn't inoculate me."

"Why?"

"Because I came down with it first. I had it already."

"So then, why should you blame Doctor Warren?"

"I don't blame him. But he's not God. Not like you think." She picked up her cap and shawl and made ready to leave the room.

"You tricked me," I said.

"How so?"

"You pushed me into thinking he was carrying on with Rachel so I would turn against him."

"You tricked yourself, Sarah. You think you're so grown-up. You have no idea of what it means. Take some advice from me, little sister. Know what you're about. Like I do. I know I'm no beauty. But at least I'm not languishing over someone old enough to be my father. And don't let anyone influence what you think. That's what being grown-up is about, after all."

Then she went out the door. I sat on the bed, hearing her footsteps pattering downstairs.

She was right. I wasn't grown-up. And because I'd tried to act like it, I'd ruined everything. I'd hurt Doctor Warren, a good and true friend. I'd seen the pain in his eyes last Sunday when I would not respond to his greeting.

I would make it right, I decided. I would say something to him. But what? And how could I ever make it right again? No matter what I said, things would never be the same with us.

There was not only pain in his eyes when he looked at me. There was disappointment. I'd seen that, too.

No, I decided, I would wait it out. I would wait until the proper moment. And then I would prove to him that I was not the silly child he thought me to be.

So I stayed home and watched the little children and baby Joshua that day.

Doctor Warren gave a stirring oration. And I missed it.

He took a chance even going. So did Father, Sam Adams, John Hancock, and all the others. There was gossip on the streets that General Gage was going to allow them to hold the celebration and then arrest his enemies on the spot.

There were no arrests, though at least forty British officers showed up and Sam Adams gave them the best seats.

No arrests, but there was a near riot. Debby told me about it that night as we lay in our beds.

"Warren gave a wonderful speech! Some British officers sat on the steps leading to the pulpit. If Warren had said one word too many against the king, they were ready to arrest him. Then Sam Adams suggested plans be made for next year's celebration of the 'bloody massacre'." Some British officers yelled, 'fie, fie'—people thought it was *fire* and there was a great rush to get out. Oh, you should have *been* there!"

"I'm glad I wasn't."

Debby lost her new mobcap. And her shawl. She was upset over that. She loved her finery and had quite a bit of it. Grandmother was always making or purchasing it for her. Always I'd been jealous, because I had to wear her hand-me-downs.

After what she'd told me this morning, though, I knew I would never be jealous of her again. Still, I had all I could do to keep from saying, "It serves you right."

Chapter Twelve

$\mathcal{T}$HE FIRST WEEK in April, something happened in our house that I don't ever remember happening before.

Father had an argument with Grandmother.

This was no trifling business, either. It started when Grandmother set his plate of eggs and fish down before him. She made Father's breakfast every morning. It had always been her job, and Rachel did not take it away from her. Besides, Rachel was busy with the baby. The rest of us were eating.

"When are we leaving?" Grandmother asked.

"Leaving for where?" Father answered absent-mindedly.

"For Concord. With the rest of them."

"The rest of whom?" Father asked innocently.

Grandmother put her hands on her hips. "Don't play like you don't know, Paul. Your Whig friends. The ones Gage has orders to arrest."

"We don't know that Gage has orders to arrest anybody."

"Bah," Grandmother said. "Your people knew the contents of those letters that came in from England on those ships at Marblehead the other day. Knew what they said before Gage did. And that's why they've all fled. And left you and Warren here, cornered."

Father smiled and ate leisurely. "Yes, we knew, Mother. It's our job to know such things."

"So it's true, then."

"Gage isn't going to arrest anybody," Father said.

Grandmother glared at him. The rest of us, from Paul down to Mary, sat entranced. Even little Joshua in Rachel's arms stared, sensing something.

"Anyone in Boston who is a Patriot and has any brains is on the move," Grandmother said.

"Well, I suppose that leaves me out then," Father returned.

"Don't joke, Paul. Think of your family. John Hancock left yesterday in that fancy carriage of his. With his aunt Lydia, her niece Dorothy, and his secretary. Going to Lexington, I hear. To Jonas Clarke's house."

Father sipped some coffee and eyed her. "We ought to have you on our Committee of Safety, Mother. You gather information better than anyone."

"Bah!" She sat down and helped herself to fish and eggs. "Sam Adams is gone, too."

"He's gone to the Provincial Congress," Father said.

"The Provincial Weaklings, you mean."

That was too much for Father. He set his mug down with a clatter. "Now you overstep yourself, Mother. Sam Adams has remade the colonial legislature into the Provincial Congress. A body of men who govern themselves, with no ties to England. So hush."

She did not hush. "Hancock thinks enough of his aunt Lydia to get her out of Boston."

"If you want to leave, Mother, I'll make provision for it."

"Did I say I wanted to leave?"

"Then what is this all about?"

"It is about you having some common sense. And thinking of your family."

Father looked around the table, from one of us to the other. "Is there any member of my family who would like to voice an opinion about leaving Boston?"

No one answered. "Well?" he asked.

In turn, each of his children said no.

"Don't ask the children," she said. "They don't know what's acting. You do."

"Rachel?" Father asked. "Do you fear for your family?"

"No, Paul. I fear for you. When you go on your rides. But I know we'll be fine so long as you're here."

"Bah!" Grandmother said.

Father and Paul left for the shop then. And when I took Father his noon meal, he was in a dour mood. And he took it out on me.

FATHER KEPT the shop door closed these days. Paul was out delivering an elaborate bill head

Father had designed and engraved for Joshua Brackett, owner of the Cromwell Head Inn.

I went alone to the shop because Debby was helping Rachel and Grandmother air out the carpets and mattresses on this lovely spring day.

No sooner was I inside the door when there was a rapping on it. Doctor Warren stood there.

"Open it," Father said.

I did so and stepped aside.

"I've come for my teeth," Warren said.

"They're ready," Father told him. "I'll wire them in now. Come to the back room."

"Thank heavens. I know I'm vain, but I miss the eyetooth. Never again will I eat a hazelnut. Hello, Sarah."

I nodded but did not answer. Hostility lay between me and Warren, thicker than the sawdust on the floor.

"Haven't you a tongue in your head?" Father asked.

"Don't scold," Warren admonished him.

"I'll scold if I wish. The women in my family are getting the upper hand these days."

Warren said something about women always having the upper hand. That men just didn't realize it. And they went into the back room. But not before Father turned to level a stern gaze at me. "Don't leave, Sarah. I don't like you walking the streets alone. Doctor Warren will see you home."

"I can manage," I argued. "All the soldiers are busy repairing tents and laying out field equipment. They scarce paid me mind."

"Wait, I say." My father's voice brooked no argument.

I waited. And I listened to their voices from the back room.

"By heaven, you shouldn't go about making night visits anymore, Joseph," Father was saying. "I fear you'll be ambushed."

"I won't let my patients suffer because of these rascally British," Warren said.

"Then take one of your medical students with you."

"A medical student? They are of a mind that we shouldn't stand up for our rights. The young weaklings! By God, I hope I die up to my knees in blood! We must fight for our rights as Englishmen!"

Englishmen? I thought. Then Father spoke.

"Stop talking so I can wire these teeth in, Joseph. Then utter no more words about dying."

DOCTOR WARREN walked me home. There was nothing for it. I had to do as Father wished.

What shall I say to him? I asked myself. *Now is the time to make things right between us.*

But I could not do it.

We walked in silence along Clark's Wharf. It was a fine April day. Gulls cried and dipped overhead. The smell of the water from the harbor was the smell of life itself in Boston.

But Warren saw no life today. Only death. "Never thought the day would come when British warships would occupy this harbor, and not our own trading vessels," he said.

He brooded the matter. I cast a sidelong glance at him. Did he consider himself an Englishman, then? Or an American? Did he know? All that talk about dying in blood frightened me.

It came to me then that he'd likely forgotten our argument. After all, he had more important things on his mind.

He and Father were the leading Whigs left in Boston. Father said Sam Adams had left Warren in charge.

So he had things of importance on his mind. They must have weighed heavily on him, for we were off the wharf and on Fish Street before he spoke again. "Like the rest of us, your father is anxious these days."

It was his way of saying I should not take Father's vile mood to heart. Right then I should have said, *No, he was right. I've been rude to you for too long now.*

But I didn't say it, weakling that I was. "Grandmother has been plaguing him to leave Boston," I said instead. "She says Gage is going to arrest him."

"Gage will make no arrests. He's no fool. He knows us as Parliament doesn't. How could they know us? Gage is mindful that if he arrests one of us, ten more will take that man's place."

I felt reassured. And we continued our walk in silence. At our door, I thanked him, most properlike. "Will you come in?"

"No, I must run. Tell Rachel and your grandmother not to worry. When the time comes, I'll see that your father and his family get out of Boston."

And what about you? I wanted to ask. But I

didn't. I thanked him. The air between us was constrained.

He gave a little half-bow and turned to go.

Wait, I wanted to say. *Wait, please, and let's talk of what really lies between us. Before it is too late.*

Too late for what, I did not know. But I felt time pressing down on my shoulders. I stood at our door and watched him walk away, a tall, distinguished-looking man. Yet ever so boyish looking at times. And he had the weight, here in Boston, of the whole rebellion on his shoulders.

His figure was etched for me clearly in the bright April sun. Some British soldiers on the street greeted him, and he nodded and waved. Even General Gage, we heard, knew he was a man to be reckoned with. For all Warren's talk about dying up to his knees in blood, he'd met cordially with Gage and they respected one another.

His surgery had become the headquarters for Boston Whigs these days. As much as Province House and Gage's office were the meeting place for the British.

What secrets, then, about the rebellion did he

carry in his head and his heart that no one else knew?

And with all of it, how did he regard me? Gentleman that he was, he'd avoided the subject, though he knew bad cess lay between us.

He respected the feelings of a little slip of a girl as much as those of General Gage. Tears crowded my eyes as I went into the house.

WE HAD two arguments in our house that week. It was becoming like the province itself. Torn apart. I wondered how many other households in Boston were having the same problem.

Debby started the second argument.

At the end of the first week in April, there was a flurry of activity in Boston Harbor. In full view of the citizens, longboats were being launched from British men-of-war. The longboats were moored directly under the sterns of the great ships.

The people nearly went crazy with speculation. Rumors flew. Everyone was convinced that the British were ready to launch an offensive.

But where?

"Concord," my brother Paul said.

He was anxious to make up to Father for the misinformation he'd brought home about Castle Island. Paul often stayed late at the shop these spring nights. People knew him because he made deliveries for Father.

Stable boys knew him. Some of them worked for the British.

"Gage has heard there are military stores at Concord," Paul said at supper. It was Friday, the seventh, the day the British launched the boats.

Father only nodded. He and Paul went after supper to Warren's office. And the next day, Father rode to warn the people of Concord.

Before his return on Sunday, British soldiers in the street were greeting Paul with jocularity. "Is your father back yet?"

Gage knew my father was gone to warn the people of Concord.

"It's Church," Paul told Father once again, when Father was sitting down to a hard-earned meal late Sunday. "I'd make a wager on it."

"He's in Concord," Father said.

"He could have sent a rider back to Gage. It's only twenty-one miles."

I looked at my brother. He'd sprouted up this spring. His shoulders had widened. His face had become lean. His dark eyes did nothing but question these days. Fear gnawed at my innards.

Paul was becoming a man. Fast. Previously we'd only had to worry about Father in this house. Did we now have to worry about Paul, too? I thought of Mother. Paul had been her baby boy. What would she think of him now?

"Doctor Church is a member of the Provincial Congress. And the Committee of Safety," Father reminded him. But his face was white, his lips grim.

All of this talk was what led Debby to her argument.

"Mayhap it's someone else," she said. She was sitting at the end of the table, doing some crewel-work. "All kinds of people come into *this* house."

Father's soupspoon paused midair. "What are you saying, my girl?"

"Well, what about Lady Frankland? She was here Saturday morning, right after you left."

"Are we to concern ourselves with this again?" Father asked.

Debby tossed her head. "I have never stopped concerning myself with it."

In the other room, Rachel was nursing Joshua. The children were playing in the yard.

Grandmother, in her usual corner by the hearth, apparently dozing, opened her eyes.

Father lowered his voice. "Suspicion is tearing Boston apart," he said. "I'll not have it do its dirty work in this house."

"You're too late, Father." Debby picked up her needlework and made ready to leave the room. "It already has."

"Just a moment, miss."

Debby stopped.

Father looked at Paul. "Have you reason to suspect Lady Frankland?"

"No, sir. The British soldiers all laugh at her. They call her—" Paul stopped.

"Yes?" Father asked.

"Not a nice name." My brother's eyes slid to me and he blushed.

"They call her a whore," Debby said. "Which she is."

"That is enough!" Father's benign face got red, as it did when he became angry. Which wasn't often. "Debby, if you use such language again, I shall be forced to question and curtail your associations."

"I'm sorry, Father. I won't." She knew he meant Amos.

"Furthermore, I say that Lady Frankland is to be allowed in this house. And treated with the utmost respect. By all. Is that understood, Debby?"

"Yes." But she was pouting.

"Mother?" And he turned to look at her. She had closed her eyes and was pretending sleep.

That week, on the fifteenth, we had just sat to supper when Paul came rushing into the house. "Gage has taken his grenadiers and light infantry off duty. Word is he has something important for them to do."

"Let's see what's acting," Father said. He and Paul went out. And when we woke on Sunday morning he was gone.

"He's off to Lexington," Paul told Rachel. "To carry the news about the grenadiers and light infantry to Hancock and Adams."

Rachel paled, then rallied. "We shall conduct the Sabbath as always. Children, come to breakfast. Then we go to meeting."

In the afternoon, Lady Frankland came to call.

"You see?" Debby whispered. "She's here again! She always knows when Father is off on a ride!"

Lady Frankland came sweeping in, bearing

gifts. A new primer for Frances and Mary, a rag doll for Elizabeth. And freshets of news. She was dressed in varying shades of blue. Her silver-white hair was piled high in the mode of the day. Her perfume filled the room.

"My dears! I am so sorry to come unannounced! But I leave today for my country place, Frankland Hall in Hopkinton." She embraced Rachel. "I shall miss you. You must come and pay a visit. Oh, I shall miss you, my dear friend."

Rachel said she would, though I doubted the likelihood of it.

Lady Frankland held out her arms for baby Joshua. "I just met Mary Thomas, wife of the printer. Her husband is sending her and the children to Watertown."

"Two children whose paternity can never be made sure of," Grandmother said from her chair.

"Be that as it may, the poor dear was in tears. She says Gage is going to seize her husband's press and arrest him for treason."

"He ought to arrest her. For consorting," Grandmother said.

"Debby, make up some coffee, please," Rachel put in. "Come, sit, Agnes. In the parlor."

"I was about to go out," Debby said.

Rachel turned. "Where?"

"I'm meeting Amos."

"Where are you going?" Rachel asked. "The streets are full of soldiers."

"To Griffin's Wharf. To see Captain Oliver De Lancey. He's arrived on the *Nautilus.* Did you hear anything about that, Lady Frankland?" Debby's sweetness was contrived.

"Oh, yes, I *saw* him on my way here. My dear! He was most dashing. What a uniform!"

"It's the Seventeenth Light Dragoons," Paul said.

"But his cavalry helmet had a grinning death's head and crossbones on it," Lady Frankland said. "I do think that rather absurd, don't you?"

"I think it rather fitting," Debby said.

That brought Lady Frankland up short. She stared at Debby, who returned the look with practiced sauciness.

"He's Mrs. Gage's American cousin," my sister said. "In the service of the king." Her words were heavy with meaning.

"Yes." Lady Frankland stood cuddling Joshua. "But Margaret has no claim on him."

"Doesn't she?" Debby reached for her cap and tossed her head. "Strange. I'd heard otherwise."

"Debby!" Rachel snapped.

"Yes?"

"You will keep a civil tongue in your head."

"It's all right," Lady Frankland said. "Tell me, Debby, do you have some concern about me? If you do, speak it plain."

Debby did. "You wear lovely perfume, Lady Frankland. But soon people will want to know if that is a fragrance or a stink."

"Debby!" Rachel was horrified.

"No," Lady Frankland said, "let her continue, please."

"Are you a Tory at heart?" my sister asked. "Or American?"

"I'll make coffee," I said quickly.

"I'm going out for a few minutes, Rachel," Paul said. "Major Pitcairn, who's quartered with the Shaws, is forming up his light companies. I want to see how many men he's got."

It was not like Paul to announce what information he might gather for Father. But I knew what he was doing, and I loved him for it.

He was giving his trust to Lady Frankland.

"Paul?" she called to him.

He stopped at the door. "Yes, ma'am?"

"You may want to know this. That nice Mrs. Stedman has as a housemaid the wife of one Private Gibson. His sergeant was rounding up his men and came looking for Gibson. He told Mrs. Stedman that Gibson should be at the bottom of the Common at eight o'clock tonight. Equipped for an expedition."

For only a moment, Paul's dark eyes, which did nothing but question these days, shone with satisfaction. "Thank you," he said.

Lady Frankland leveled a calm look at Debby. Then she turned to Rachel. "Shall we go into the parlor and visit?"

My sister tossed her head, pushed past Paul, who was holding the door open, and went out.

"Oh, I shall miss you, Rachel," Lady Frankland was saying again. "I do so love Frankland Hall, but I shall miss you and Margaret Gage and all my friends."

Chapter Thirteen

*R*ACHEL TOLD me and Paul that there would be no profit in telling Father what Debby had done. "To what aim?" she asked. "Your father has more on his mind these days than a body should. Lady Frankland put her in her place and the matter is finished." And she told me later, "Besides, Lady Frankland will be away all summer. Things will simmer down before she is back."

I thought it fitting. We were a family of secrets. One more couldn't hurt.

Sunday evening was lovely. There was a golden pinkness to the sunset. The air smelled

of the earth, the sea, and the presence of spring.
Father returned jovial. And all seemed peaceful
as we gathered around the table in the dining
room. Ordinary street sounds came through the
open windows. Birds twittered. Daffodils grew
outside our back door; a lilac bush bloomed in
the yard.

One could pretend it was Boston as it should
be. No General Gage, no soldiers on the street,
no orders from England to arrest a body for just
wanting to be what he wanted to be.

We had a saddle of lamb, I recollect, new potatoes, vegetables, milk punch, bread and cheese,
and pie.

Father was talking about the people he'd seen
on his trip. And telling us how lovely the countryside was in spring. And how Boston looked
from Charlestown across the water.

"A grand city," he said. "I felt a tug at my
heart when I saw the steeple of Christ Church.
It's Boston's tallest building, you know."

"You walked the steps to that steeple many a
time when you were a boy," Grandmother told
him.

It was the first time she'd spoken to him since
their argument.

"Yes, I did," Father said. And for the moment he seemed sad. He pushed his food around on his plate.

"I still have that paper you and those boys signed for your Bell Ringers Society," Grandmother said.

"Ah yes," Father said. "We rang the bells for two hours every week."

"In an Episcopal church." Grandmother laughed. "Your father wanted to thrash you when he found out. I said, 'Let the boy earn his shilling. Let the Episcopals pay him for his industry.' "

Father smiled sourly. "Do you know how many steps there are up to that steeple, children?"

Of course we did. We'd heard the story before. How my father, a dirty little urchin apprenticed to a goldsmith, rang the bells in Old North with other boys to earn shillings.

"One hundred and fifty-four," said Frances.

"Good girl!" Father was delighted.

Something happened then that I shall never forget.

The bells of Christ Church, commonly called Old North, started to ring their evensong.

At first the sound was distant and delicate. But soon it carried, sweet and haunting, on the evening air.

Everyone fell silent. I saw tears in Father's eyes.

"They dispel demons," Grandmother whispered. "My Paul was up there in that steeple dispelling demons when he was just a lad. It's the reason I've always loved those bells."

Father took out a square of cloth and blew his nose. "I pray they could," he said. Then he spoke again. "The tallest building in Boston." He shook his head. "How couldn't you dispel demons from there?"

We didn't know what he was thinking, of course. How could we? No more than we could know that this was the last time we would sit together and sup in this house of a Sunday evening for a whole year.

I suppose I wasn't surprised two days later on Tuesday, the eighteenth, when the pounding came on our door. Rachel had taken the children out for an airing. Grandmother was upstairs in her room, spinning some thread. Paul was in the shop with Father. I was home alone, making cookies.

I opened the door. A ragged boy stood there. The look in his eyes was one of sheer terror, as if the devil himself was pursuing him. His breath was spent.

Nevertheless, he managed to get out the words that were to change our lives forever.

"Got a message for Mr. Revere."

"He's not home. But I can take it."

"Tell him there's gonna be the hell to pay to-morrow."

"What do you mean?"

He bent over, hands on his knees, to catch his breath. "My friend works in a stable where the regulars keep their horses. He says they been talkin'. Tomorrow they're gonna raise hell at Concord. Go after the military stores."

"How can I be sure you're not bringing my father false information?" My brother had told me to ask this question. We had been expecting this today because Gage had been sending officers out to the countryside to stop alarm riders.

After Father's trip two days ago, most of the

military stores were moved from Concord. But large stocks of provisions were still there, along with some cannon and gunpowder.

The boy straightened up and wiped his nose with his sleeve. "Me and my friend. We act like we support the Crown."

I said nothing.

"Would I run all the way from Province House like this for false information?"

Still I said nothing.

"Tell you this," he said. "Gage's men been seen on country roads, wearin' heavy coats with holsters an' swords under 'em."

"We know that."

"They been talkin' to people in the country taverns. Askin' the whereabouts of Hancock and Adams."

I felt the intake of my breath. "We didn't know that," I said.

"An' you know where his officers been all mornin'? On Long Wharf. Meetin' and talkin'. 'Cause that's the only place in town where Yankee ears can't pick up on anythin'."

"All right," I said. "Wait here." I went into the house and came out with a shilling, as I knew

Paul would do. Then I put my cookies in the beehive oven and waited for Rachel.

"So it's come, then." Rachel settled the children at the table. I got out their wooden bowls. Grandmother came down from her room. I spooned soup into the bowls from a pot bubbling on the hearth. It was just noon.

Through the windows came the high-pitched boatswain's pipes aboard the warships in the harbor.

We all listened. "They're up to mischief," Grandmother said. "I hope they're happy now, John Hancock and his aunt Lydia." What they had to do with things, I didn't know, but she lay all blame at their feet.

"I was in the apothecary shop," Rachel said, "for headache powders. A British officer was there, dressed for battle."

"Yes," I said. "I suppose it's come."

We stared at each other, Rachel and I. What did we mean by "it"?

The end of all the months of preparation, of waiting, of secrets, of conspiring, of arguing and uncertainty in our house, surely. I almost felt relieved. But if all that was at an end and "it" was now upon us, what could we look to now?

"Well, whatever's coming, I've still got to water my seedlings," Grandmother said. And she took a pitcher and went out to the well.

"You'd best go give your father the message." Rachel set a sleeping Joshua down in his cradle.

"What if I don't, Rachel? What if we just don't tell him? Just this once?"

She was kneeling over baby Joshua. She looked up. And I knew she was taken with the idea. "Oh Sarah," she said. She said it sad and she said it with a voice old with wisdom.

"Just this *once?*"

"Oh Sarah." Tears came into her eyes. She stood up. "Do you think I haven't wanted the same thing? Haven't thought of the same thing? More than once?"

I nodded. "I suppose it wouldn't do any good," I said. "Doctor Warren will send for him anyway."

"It won't do any good because of what your father *is*, Sarah. When I first met him I thought, we will have a good life. He is a good man. He loves his family. Then when I knew him a while I thought, we will not have such a good life. *Because* he is a good man and loves his family."

I nodded, but I did not understand.

"He wants this *thing*, Sarah. This public liberty. He has the notion for it. Not only for himself. But for his children."

I nodded again, this time understanding. Then I went out the door and into the street to tell my father.

"I'VE HAD two other such messages this day," Father said, looking up from the worktable in his shop.

Paul was in a corner polishing a small silver picture frame. He did not look up.

"What will you do, Father?"

"Nothing. Until I'm asked."

"You mean by Doctor Warren, don't you?"

"He's the one doing the asking these days."

"Is he going to send you to Concord?"

"When he comes by the right information, likely."

"But Gage has men out on all the roads waiting to capture you."

He smiled again. "Do you think, Sarah, that

we do not have our plans? Oh, by the way, you remember Mr. Dawes, don't you?"

Only then did a young man step out of the back room of the shop. His presence startled me. The way he hovered in the background put me on notice. There seemed to be something between him and Father and Paul.

It came to me then. *They had been plotting. And I had interrupted them.*

"Yes," I said. "Hello, Mr. Dawes." He was young, in his early twenties, a tanner from the North End. He did not run with Father and the other leading Whigs, but recently he had knocked down a British sentry for insulting his very pretty wife. He was cocky and sure of himself. He had a long nose and close-set eyes.

He bowed to me.

I thought there was a bit of mockery in it.

"Will you be home on time for supper?" I asked Father.

"No. Tell Rachel I'll be a bit late. As soon as dusk falls I'm going to help Isaiah Thomas get his printing press into a small boat and out of Boston."

He said it lightly, without concern, and went

on working. So did Paul. Dawes just stood against the doorjamb to the other room, arms folded across his middle, smiling.

They were waiting for me to leave so they could go on plotting. But I lingered, pondering. I knew enough about my father's doings to understand that smuggling a printing press out of Boston was serious business.

I went over to the worktable of a sudden and kissed him.

"What's this?" He smiled at me. "Are you all right, my lamb?"

"Yes. But I want you to be."

"And why shouldn't I be?"

"Because I heard the talk that Gage is going to arrest Thomas and smash his press. Be careful."

"Aren't I always? What's to eat tonight?"

"Fish stew."

"Tell Rachel to keep it warm."

I left the shop knowing that whatever Father was planning, Dawes was in on it. Likely he was helping Father tonight. And that was better. Because up to now, he hadn't been active in their doings. And the British would not recognize him.

WE ALWAYS KNEW—I, Rachel, Paul, and Debby—that the time would come when Father would ride out of Boston and not come back. Not to Boston as we knew it, not to our life as we knew it.

When it happened, finally, it seemed the natural order of things. It even seemed right. As things can come to seem right that are not so. Because we have been led to believe it.

Only he didn't ride out of Boston. He walked. Warren sent for him that very night, late.

By dusk we knew he would go. Troops were assembling at the bottom of the Common, where the longboats were drawn up. Everyone knew it. The people watched them.

We did not go to bed that night. Not even the children. They had been put to bed but were giggling and running about upstairs, their bare feet pattering on the wooden floors. Several times either Debby or I had to go up and quiet them.

The rest of us sat and waited. Debby and I did our sewing. Rachel was making tomorrow's bread dough. Finally, Grandmother went to bed. Paul sat in a corner polishing his musket, and Father was reading.

From outside came the sound of troops

assembling on the cobblestones, the clanking of muskets, the sharp bark of their officers.

We did not speak of this but of sundry everyday things. We drew close around the kitchen hearth, seeking warmth and comfort from one another. For the world out in North Square had turned hostile.

Then, of a sudden, Father put his newspaper down. "Don't take that musket out on the streets, Paul, promise me."

Paul nodded.

"And if I am not here and things act up, you may have to turn it over to the king's men."

"I'll not do that," Paul said.

"You must if it is required. Don't do anything to bring their wrath down on this family. We've talked about that now, Paul, haven't we?"

Paul nodded.

"Debby, you're to mind Rachel. And you and Sarah look after the little ones."

I missed a stitch on the pillow slip I was embroidering and stuck my finger. Blood appeared on the white cotton. I stared at it. My mouth was dry.

"I think," Father said, "that I'll go upstairs now and bid them good night."

Rachel went with him. The rest of us sat in silence. But only for a moment. No sooner had they mounted the steps than a soft knock came on the back door. It was ten o'clock.

Paul opened it. Outside all was dank and misty. "Yes?"

A boy stood there. "I've a message from Doctor Warren."

Paul stepped outside and was back a moment later. "Debby, pack some food for him," he said. And he went upstairs to find Father.

How MUCH did Paul know? He did not speak much anymore. He moved in his own sphere these days, confiding in no one, talking in low tones to Father. They spoke to each other in half-sentences. As if in some kind of code.

It was Paul who readied Father's things while Father was gone to Doctor Warren's. Paul who told us what he would need.

After about an hour, in which I thought I would jump out of my skin, Father came back. He was cheerful, rubbing his hands, saying what a fine night it was for a ride and, yes, he'd have a bowl of soup before he left.

"Where do you ride?" Rachel asked.

He sipped his soup. "Lexington. Warren has word from a special informer that Gage is out to capture Adams and Hancock. He's sent Billy Dawes, too. He's to ride north through the sentries on the Neck."

"Dawes?" Rachel gaped. "But what experience has he?"

"He's a loyal Whig. His business often takes him through the British checkpoint on the Neck. They know him."

We sat watching him eat.

"No pistols?" Rachel asked.

"A person could get hanged for exciting armed revolt, riding about the countryside this night wearing pistols," Father said.

Rachel's face was tear-streaked. "Paul, go and ready Militia."

"No Militia, either," Father said. "You can't get out of Boston on a horse this night. With Dawes it's different. They trust him. Joshua Bentley, the boatbuilder, and a friend will row me across the Charles."

"But you'll need Militia," Rachel argued. "She's speedy and surefooted."

He was pulling on his heavy boots. "They have a horse for me in Charlestown. A good

Yankee horse belonging to John Larkin. Warren has it all arranged. She's small but sure of foot, and tireless, I've been told. With a flash of wildness in her soft eyes. Even her name bespeaks her nature. Brown Beauty."

Brown Beauty. I felt a tug at my heart, saw, in my mind's eye, the brave little mare being saddled and bridled and led out of this John Larkin's barn, stamping her dainty hooves in impatience.

"Paul, I'll need some cloth to muffle the oars," he said.

"In the cupboard in the parlor," Rachel directed.

Finally he was ready. He bade us good-bye, mumbling something comforting to each, and went out into the dank air. Paul bolted the door behind him.

We were securing the house for the night. Rachel had gone to bed, so had Debby, when Paul saw Father's spurs lying there by the doorstep.

"I must bring them," he said.

"He said not to go out."

"He needs his spurs."

"Let me go with you."

"No."

"You'd be safer."

He glared at me. "How so?"

"The two of us would be only one more couple on the streets rushing off to some romantic liaison. All the soldiers will do is heckle us."

He grunted. "You'd best stop reading *Tom Jones,*" he said.

But he took me with him. The reason being his, not mine. He'd looked around and discovered that Ruffles was missing.

The dog must have slipped out the door, unbeknownst to us, and followed Father. It might take the two of us to find him.

"We'll need no excuse now," he said. "We're looking for our dog."

So we went. There was a bright moon. It came through the mist and shone off the house windows. I kept my head down and followed Paul through the back streets.

Chapter Fourteen

*H*OW MUCH did Paul know? He knew everything that night, it seemed.

He knew all the back alleys. He knew where Ruffles went when he sneaked out.

He knew where Father was meeting Joshua Bentley. At the corner of North and North Centre Streets.

We found them there—Father, Bentley, and another man. Ruffles was with them.

"Who goes there?" Bentley called out in a loud whisper.

Paul bade me hide in the shadows. Then

he answered. "A friend. And true Whig. Paul Revere." Then he went forward.

"Your spurs," he told Father.

They conferred. Paul picked up Ruffles.

"He followed me," I heard Father saying. "Good you came. Who's with you there in the shadows?"

"Sarah. We thought it best to come together. It would look like a romantic liaison. The soldiers are used to that on the streets at night."

Father laughed. It was a nervous laugh. He clapped Paul on the back, waved to me, and then consulted more with my brother. He was pointing, giving directions. Then he and the others disappeared into the darkness.

I felt a hole inside me big enough to fall into, standing there hearing their echoing footsteps.

Paul came back across the empty street. "You want to see the lanthorns, Sarah?" he asked.

"What lanthorns?"

"Father's signal lights. From the steeple of Old North. If we hurry we can see them on the way home. Come on, we'll have to double back to Fish Street, then go one block beyond our house to Cross Street so's not to be seen."

Signal lights? What signal lights? I didn't ask.

Paul was very excited and willing to make me part of this tonight, so I followed him through the empty streets. Our footsteps echoed. We met no one. Once or twice we saw a form in the distance, but not many civilians were about that night. Paul carried Ruffles.

We'd run down Ship Street and were on Fish, along the wharves, a block beyond where our house was, when he stopped and put a hand on my arm.

"There, look, Sarah."

I looked in the direction that he pointed.

High above all the buildings was the steeple of Old North. The moon rose above it. A few shredded clouds were in the sky.

And then I saw them. Father's lanthorns. They shone in the steeple. First just a flicker. And then a flash.

Two yellow beacons, burning closely together.

I shivered and moved closer to my brother. "What *are* they?"

"Signal lights. To our people in Charlestown. To let them know if the troops go by land or by sea. If they went by land, one lanthorn was to be lit. Two, if by sea."

"Who's up there in the steeple?"

"Robert Newman, the sexton. Father asked him sometime this afternoon to help hang the lanthorns. Then he met with him on the way home from Warren's tonight. Warren had just found out they were to go by sea. Captain Pulling of the North End Caucus is with Newman. Father said Newman had to sneak out the window of his mother's house to meet with Father. British officers board there, and were in the parlor playing cards."

I stared at the flickering lanthorns. They glowed brightly against the dark. Like jewels.

Father's signals.

I shivered. Tears came to my eyes and I felt a great wellspring of feeling rising inside me. A sense of wonder and pride, of being a *part* of something this night.

Something wonderful. And new. And yet unnamed. And Father and so many others that I knew and had known were part of it. I felt so filled with pride I thought my heart would burst.

I smiled at my brother. He smiled back. "Thank you for showing me," I said.

He nodded. "Thought you'd like it. Father and Warren and others have planned it well. In Charlestown they're readying his horse right now. Let's go home. We'll have to take some dark alleys. Just stay close to me and be quiet."

I followed him. When I again looked up at the steeple of Old North, it was dark. Father was somewhere in the middle of the Charles River. On the other side, the horse was waiting.

"Remember that you saw the signal lanthorns tonight." Paul's voice came from up ahead, low and husky. "Remember it and tell your children."

Chapter Fifteen

*W*hat matters? What's true? Or what people think?

Next morning, Wednesday, we had to go to school—Frances, Elizabeth, Mary, and I. Rachel wouldn't have it any other way.

"Most people don't know your father rode off. We don't want them to think anything's different in our house."

Paul had to go right to Father's shop because it couldn't be left untended. Grandmother was feeling sickly and wanted only Debby. So I was in charge of my sisters.

The streets were quiet. Everyone was going

about his or her morning affairs. And then we turned a corner right by Scollay's Building and stood stock-still.

Tremont Street, where Mrs. Tisdale ran our school, was filled with soldiers.

They were lined up. All the way down Tremont to the bottom of the Mall.

The officers were giving ringing orders. They echoed off the buildings.

My sisters clung to me. Frances was terrified. "It's all right," I said. "We can't show fear."

"Why?" Frances asked.

I did not know why. But it was what Father would have said. I was all for showing fear, myself. I wanted to turn and run home. But I knew I couldn't do that. For one thing, I wouldn't give the British soldiers the satisfaction.

Then, as if everything wasn't bad enough, the officer in charge saw us and came walking over. His polished boots sounded on the cobblestones. "Ah, the Revere girls, I take it?"

I recognized the thin, bony frame of Lord Percy, the man so admired by John Hancock's aunt Lydia. He wore a uniform of scarlet and green, trimmed with silver lace.

He bowed. "Good morning, ladies."

I mumbled a response. My sisters did not.

"And how is everyone in the Revere household this fine day?"

I told him we were fair to middling.

"Are you now? And your father?"

"He's keeping."

"After riding all night?"

I looked up into his pale, gaunt face. Lady Frankland had said he was the eldest son of the Duke of Northumberland and heir to one of the greatest fortunes in England. I didn't know, for the life of me, what Hancock's aunt saw in him. He may have a matched pair of carriage horses and the best riding horse in New England, but he looked a sorry business this morning. His eyes seemed sunken and his nose was too big.

"My father wasn't riding all night," I said.

He laughed. "My sainted aunt, I always said Americans were designing and artful. But do they commence to be so that young?"

Was it a question? I did not answer.

"Dear child, General Gage had a message from Colonel Smith at five o'clock this morning. Smith met with Major Mitchell in Cambridge at three. Mitchell informed him that the whole countryside is alarmed. And that he had taken the noted Paul Revere prisoner."

Frances clung to me and sobbed.

"You're frightening my sister," I told him.

His smile was dour. "Mitchell was obliged to let him go. But *don't tell me* your father wasn't riding all night, miss. What is your name again?"

"Sarah."

"Don't *tell* me that, Miss Sarah. It upsets me. For he *was*. He was out and alarming the countryside. Guns were fired. Bells rang. Drums beat to arms. It is why I and my men have been sent for. Why we are assembled in the streets at this ungodly hour."

He extended a red-sleeved arm to embrace his troops.

"Three regiments of British infantry. The Fourth, otherwise known as the King's Own. Nobody shilly-shallies with the King's Own."

Again he extended the arm. "The Forty-seventh Foot. Thoughtlessly dubbed the Cauliflowers because of the white facings on their coats. But they have brilliantly distinguished themselves in the conquest of Quebec. And the Twenty-third Royal Welch Fusiliers, who acquitted themselves honorably at Namur, Blenheim, Ramillies, Oudenaarde, Malplaquet, and Minden."

My sisters were staring at him. Little Mary had her thumb in her mouth. They were so fascinated that they had forgotten their fear.

One would be hard put to stop him now. Some of his officers were watching.

"The Royal Artillery and the Royal Marines." He smiled. "Tell me, Miss Sarah, if you will, that we will have a time of it putting down these country bumpkins. But do *not* tell me your father was not out riding last night."

I glared up at him. There was silence in the streets. Now all his officers were watching. So were some passersby. And his men heard, too, though they were made to look straight ahead, as soldiers must.

I wanted to kick him. I wanted to slap his arrogant face. But I did not. Instead I raised my chin and looked him in the eye. "I'll not tell you that, sir. But I will tell you something."

"Pray, do. I would like to hear what the daughter of this noted Paul Revere has to say this day, now that her father's actions have roused our whole garrison and broken the king's peace."

"You may be the son of the Duke of Northumberland. I don't know what that all means. We don't hold with titles here. But I do know you are the rudest person ever to draw breath!"

And with that I gathered my little sisters about me. "Come, girls, we are late for school."

WE WATCHED them go from behind the shutters of our schoolroom window.

"Children, don't make any noise. And don't get too close to the window," Mrs. Tisdale admonished. "Oh, dear, don't let them see you." She was wringing her hands. To say she was distraught was not to do justice to her efforts. The poor lady was near to hysterics. I and some of the other older girls had to becalm her. But we managed to keep an eye on the events outside, anyway.

The barking of the officers giving orders rang in the street. Boots stamped in unison as they wheeled, muskets clanked, the great wooden wheels of the wagons carrying the six-pounder field guns rumbled.

Then the order to march. Their fifers and drummers played "Yankee Doodle," a song we had come to hate. For it mocked us. Horses whinnied. They had some ragged scouts marching with them. American Tories. My brother told me they were worse than the British, for they hated the Whigs.

Regimental colors snapped in the morning breeze. And so they marched, Percy on his fancy horse at their lead. We watched them go and I thought, *My father started all this.* I could scarce keep my mind on my work all morning for thinking of it.

WE WERE dismissed early because Mrs. Tisdale had one of her sick headaches. On the way home, the streets were quiet again. I watched my little sisters skipping ahead of me.

"Sarah? Sarah Revere?"

On a corner near our house, Mr. James Bowdoin hailed me. He was an elderly man. One of Father's North End Caucus people, a rich merchant who had once been in the House of Representatives. He had been elected to the congress in Philadelphia, but had refused to go and leave his sick wife. Instead, he had donated his four chestnut horses and splendid coach to take the other delegates from Massachusetts to Philadelphia.

"Good day to you, Sarah. How's everyone at home?"

"We're fair to middling, sir."

"Sarah, I won't ask about your father. I have an idea what's happened." He stopped for a moment to cough, then commenced talking. "Sarah, my health is low. As is my wife's. For that reason I am staying on in Boston. I doubt if Gage will send one of his corporals to arrest me. He knows there will be another knock on my door one day soon and another corporal from a higher power will call."

I shivered and kept my eyes on my sisters, who were jumping over puddles just ahead.

"Tell your stepmother, Sarah, that I will act as the remaining Whig in Boston after Doctor Warren leaves."

I stared at him. "Doctor Warren is leaving?"

"He must, dear child. This very day. Or Gage will have him arrested."

I felt my face go white.

"As the remaining Whig, I will petition Gage to give safe conduct to any Americans who want to leave. Tell Rachel I shall give the man no peace until all who want to leave are permitted to do so. And that she may depend upon me to help her in any circumstances."

My heart was thudding. I only half-comprehended his words. "Thank you, sir, I'll tell her."

Doctor Warren leaving? I felt a buzzing in my ears. He *couldn't* leave. Father was gone. Warren couldn't leave, too!

I was so distraught, I almost forgot to ask after Bowdoin's wife. When I did, he proceeded to tell me about her in length. I had to beg off. "My sisters are jumping in the puddles, sir. Give my best to Mrs. Bowdoin."

I did not even know there were tears coming down my face as we ran home.

Chapter Sixteen

*W*HEN WE GOT HOME Doctor Warren was there, but he was upstairs with Grandmother, seeing to her illness. His saddlebags were strapped on to his horse, which was tethered in our yard. My sisters ran to gather sweet grass for it.

"Is he leaving?" I put the question to Debby, the only one in the kitchen.

"Yes." She was stirring a pot on the hearth.

"But why? If he goes, the Whig cause goes in Boston."

"It's gone in Boston." She was ladling some

stew into a bowl. She set it down on the table with some bread and cheese.

I felt the world moving under my feet. I had nothing solid under me. "Who will look out for us?"

Just then came the sound of footsteps on the stairs. "Don't make a fool of yourself over him," Debby whispered.

Warren and Rachel came into the kitchen. "Just keep her warm and see that she gets plenty of rest," he told Rachel. "I have an idea this has to do as much with worry as with aching bones."

He nodded to me, set down his doctor's bag, and took a chair at the table. "Thank you, Debby," he said.

I stood to one side and watched him eat. His tousled fair hair tumbled over his eyes. The tallness of him, the grace of him, the span of his shoulders, the way he held his head, were all etched in my mind.

I ached, watching him and listening to his voice as he carried on a conversation with Rachel, who was busying herself around him.

They spoke of when and how Father might get word to us of his whereabouts, of how Father had ridden all night, warning town after town before his capture, how town leaders, in turn, sent other riders out with the message.

"My messenger said he arrived in Lexington between midnight and one," Warren said. "After the British let him go."

"The horse was good, then," Rachel said.

"The best."

"And so now the shooting has started."

"Yes," Warren said. "At Lexington."

Rachel brought a bowl of batter to the table and sat down with it on her lap.

"Where will you go?" Rachel asked.

"Cambridge, I think. I'm taking the ferry."

"To doctor?"

"If need be. But more to see what needs doing with the Committee of Safety. They stood, Rachel. Our men stood at Lexington. They faced up to the redcoats, every boy and man of them. Last I heard, the redcoats were marching to Concord."

"Is this what you wanted, then?" she asked him.

"No. You know what I wanted, Rachel. I wanted our rights restored as Englishmen. Not a break with England."

She sighed. "Well, we have it now, haven't we?"

"Yes."

"Who will care for your practice here?"

"I've left it in the hands of Doctor Eustis. He'll look in on old Mrs. Revere."

They were talking in hushed tones, like—well, like *husband and wife.* As if there was some long-established understanding between them.

I spoke out. Was it from jealousy? I don't know, but I could abide it no more. "Mr. Bowdoin isn't leaving."

Doctor Warren raised his eyes slowly to me. "No, he's staying. His wife is ill. So is he."

"I met him on the way home from school. Rachel, he said to tell you that you can depend on him to help you in any circumstances."

"He's a good man," Doctor Warren said.

"Why are *you* leaving?"

Silence. And it had a deadness in it. Again he raised those sad blue eyes to me. "I must, Sarah."

"Oh, must you? Why?" I stepped forward, emboldened by my anger. "Isn't it enough that Father is gone? Who will look out for us now?"

"Sarah," Rachel admonished, "mind your tongue."

"You pretend to be such a staunch friend to this family. Father *had* to go. You don't."

"Sarah!" Rachel said again.

But there was this thing between me and Warren that had not been settled. He knew it lay there between us. And he minded it was a sick thing, as did I.

"I'll speak if I wish," I said.

"Let her speak her mind," he told Rachel.

"For heaven's sake, let the man go," Debby said. She wiped her hands on a towel. "I know you can't bear the thought, Sarah, but there are more important things he has to attend to than your childish tantrums." She threw the towel down and walked to the door. "I'll see to the children, Rachel."

I felt very much the spoiled child, standing there. Debby was right. Shots had been fired at Lexington. Men had died. More would die this day. Our world had been torn asunder. And I was pouting because Doctor Warren would no longer be around for me to languish over.

"Go on, Sarah," he said.

There was nothing for it now but to continue. So I did. "How can you think of going? You just yourself told us that Father warned the whole countryside and as a result the shooting started. Do you think the British do not know that?"

"The British will not retaliate on the families of those who led the rebellion," he said. "It is not their way."

"Not their way? Tell that to Lord Percy. In front of our school this morning, Lord Percy accosted us. Demanded to know where Father was. Mocked him. And us. And frightened the girls with his talk of Father's arrest. I would say you are needed *here*, Doctor Warren. With the people whose lives you have endangered with all your meetings and fancy orations and actions!"

"Sarah Revere!" Rachel stood up. "Your father would be sore afflicted to hear you speak so to our dear friend. Make your apologies, this minute."

I was spent. Feelings raged inside me that I could not even put a name to.

Warren said nothing for a moment. He studied his pewter soupspoon as if it held the answers to his most perplexing problems. Then he spoke. "No matter, Rachel. Everyone's in a state of agitation." He stood up and reached for his hat. "I'll take my leave now. I must catch the ferry."

Rachel walked to the door with him.

As he crossed the floor in front of me, he stopped. He looked right at me, started to speak, changed his mind, shook his head, and then did speak. "Sarah, Sarah," he said.

Just that. Then he reached out a hand.

I stepped back.

"If I could say to you what I wanted to say. But there is no time. The time is past for that."

No! I wanted to scream it at him. But I remained silent.

"Be of good heart, Sarah. What's done now is done. In Lexington and here. There is no going back. For any of us."

What did he mean by *that?*

"It's all new, Sarah. Nobody knows how to feel. We must search and find new feelings."

I glared at him. Why did I sense that he was talking about more than Lexington?

"We all must do what is given us to do in this moment. And figure the rest out later."

His voice sounded sad and old. As if he already had it figured out. But it was not given to him to divulge.

"Forget Lord Percy. For all his charm, he has not been able to stand up to circumstances. And has turned into a boorish malcontent. He is not in charge. If he gives you more trouble, go to Major Small at Province House. He is a British officer, yes, but we hold each other in high regard."

I did not reply to any of this.

"Gage will not retaliate against this family. There is an army of men assembling out there. Gage will be lucky if they don't storm Boston after what happened this day at Lexington. Gage is frightened. If I did not believe this, I would see that you all got out now. As it is, I think it is best you stay and await word from your father."

Then he went out. I watched him put the tricorn on his head, minded his fair hair tied in back, his polished boots, the way the pinned-back tails of his coat swung as he walked.

He was leaving. My world was growing cold.

They stood in the yard, talking. I saw my sisters run over to him, hug him, clamber over him. He reached into his pocket and drew out the ever-present maple sugar sweets, hugged them all, then Rachel. Then he got on his horse.

I wanted to run out and clutch at his boot, tell him I was a foolish child and I knew how terrible I was. And that he should have a care. And Godspeed.

I did none of those things. I stood and watched him ride off and I never felt so desolate in my life.

Chapter Seventeen

*F*OR THE NEXT twenty-four hours after Warren left, everything was a blur of confusion. At sunset that next day, Paul came home from the shop and said everyone was going to Beacon Hill. So we gathered the children and went, too.

We stood with the other citizens of Boston— children, elderly people leaning on canes, housewives come from their labors, whole families, even with their dogs, apprentices still in leather aprons, and some gentry—looking out across the Charles.

A blazing red sun was setting in the direction of Charlestown. It bathed us in an eerie light. It reflected on our confused faces. Across the waters we could see long lines of British Regulars marching to the riverbank, where longboats awaited them. The HMS *Somerset* was anchored midriver to receive them. Her sails caught the red of the sunset and were colored with it like blood.

We heard the distant *pop-pop-pop* of musket fire. It was from New England militiamen who had followed the Regulars all the way to Charlestown. The flashing of musket fire streaked the purple twilight.

Many of the British soldiers were being ferried back across to Boston. Others just sank down on the ground and waited. Some were carried onto boats.

"Wounded."

I heard the whispered word carried from mouth to mouth behind me.

"What does it mean?" a woman asked. "What has happened?"

"It means now there'll be hell to pay in Boston," her husband answered. No one disputed him.

"Come, children, let's go home," Rachel suggested.

At first light in the morning it started.

There came a pounding on the door. It woke me from my sleep. Then Ruffles barking. Then Rachel calling, "Paul? Paul?"

"I'll see what's acting." He sounded like my father.

I heard him putting on his boots and clumping downstairs. I got out of bed, threw on a wrap, and, in my bare feet, went into the hall to find Rachel. Debby stumbled behind me and we followed Rachel down.

"He isn't here," we heard Paul saying.

"We don't come for him. We come with a message from Province House."

"What message?" my brother asked.

"By order of Lieutenant General, the Honorable Thomas Gage, commander-in-chief of British forces in America, all weapons owned by the local citizenry are to be turned over to the selectmen, who will be ready to receive them at Province House this afternoon between one and three."

"I'll not turn over my musket," Paul said.

"Yes, he will." Rachel pushed back the long braid she wore at night and stepped forward. "Corporal?"

"Yes, ma'am?"

"He will be there."

"Rachel!" Paul whispered savagely.

She had gone to the door, stepped in front of Paul, and opened it wide. A young corporal stood there.

"Gage is doing this to prevent bloodshed, ma'am. In return, he promises that all who wish to leave will be permitted to do so."

"He will be there," Rachel said again. And she closed the door.

"Rachel, I can't turn over my firearms," Paul argued.

"You must!" she said. "We can't have this house singled out for failing to obey. We're practically under martial law. And we want to leave when your father sends for us."

"We don't even know that he's still alive." Paul's voice broke.

"He's alive!" Rachel whirled on him. Then seeing my brother's bowed head, she put her hands on his shoulders. She had to stand on tiptoe to do so. "He's alive, Paul. Very much alive. And you must do what he would do. You must act for the good of the family. We're depending on you. You're man of the house now."

That afternoon my brother went with one of

our cousins his age, Thomas Hitchbourne, to turn in two muskets. He promised Rachel he would do it without getting cheeky. He promised her he would not start trouble. But I saw, from the look in his eyes as he ran his hands lovingly over the long barrels and the gleaming brass that he so often polished, that neither would he do it without a broken heart.

He took longer at Province House than we expected. We waited supper for him, as we would for Father. I was turning a chicken on the spit. Rachel and Debby had taken Grandmother her supper. She was still in bed.

"Sarah, I've a story to tell. Wait until you hear it." Paul's eyes were dark and shining when he came in.

Rachel and Debby came down, and I ushered the little girls to the table. Paul was about to slip into his accustomed chair, but Rachel stood at the head of the table and pulled out Father's chair. "Come sit, Paul," she said.

He looked taken aback. But he sat in Father's place.

Rachel served him first, as she had done with Father.

"I have a story to tell," he said when all were served.

"Tell it," Rachel said.

"The Regulars took a beating. They marched to Concord—to where the stores were—after they fired on the farmers at Lexington. But the stores were hidden, thanks to Father's warnings. The farmers in Concord faced the Regulars on a bridge and chased them."

"Any dead?" Rachel asked.

Paul nodded yes. "Other militia arrived. From Lincoln, Carlisle, Chelmsford, Bedford, Acton, Westford, Watertown, Weston, they came. From Worcester, Portsmouth, Marblehead, even Connecticut. Thousands of them came pouring over the fields. The British line broke, and they ran."

We listened as our food got cold on our plates.

"The Regulars gathered in Concord town. Our militia watched from the hills. Then the Regulars started back to Boston."

He looked at Mary, Frances, and Elizabeth, who were listening as if to a bedtime story. "How many miles from Concord to Boston?"

"Sixteen," Frances said.

"Good, good." Paul smiled. "So they had sixteen miles to go. And our militia followed. Not in columns, like the British march, all smart and pretty, with colors flying and fifes and drums playing. No, our militia crept along ridges and ducked low in open meadows. And hid behind fences and houses and barns and stone walls. And all the while, all the *while* the Regulars were marching on that road, other militia were coming through the fields. From Reading and Billerica and Tewksbery. From all the little towns all over."

Paul dropped his voice to a whisper. The little girls had their mouths open. It was a story. Rachel smiled.

Paul went on. "The Regulars were tired and hungry. They tramped and tramped. Then, of a sudden, came a musket shot. How does it sound, Second Mary?"

"Bop," she said.

"Yes, *bop,*" Paul agreed. "And *bop* and *bop.* From our militia. From behind fences and trees, from drainage ditches and behind rocks. From out of windows. Of a sudden the Regulars would look up, and there on a hill, like ghosts, would be a thousand militia, just standing there, waiting for them. They fired on the Regulars, *bop* and *bop* and *bop*."

"What happened?" Elizabeth asked.

"They had a score to settle, our militia. And they did it. On one hill was Captain Parker with his company of men the British had shot into on Lexington Common that morning. They hit Colonel Smith in the thigh. And so it went, all the way back to Boston. Our militia gave no quarter. They followed, they stalked the Regulars all the way back to Charlestown. They were led by General Heath, a farmer from Roxbury. And by someone else we know."

"Father!" Elizabeth said.

"No, not Father." Paul's dark eyes sought mine across the table. "By Doctor Warren. I heard"—he leaned forward and whispered it to the little girls—"I heard that it was Warren's decision to follow the Regulars all the way back to Boston."

They clapped and cheered. Debby gave me a snide glance.

"There was Warren. On horseback. Under enemy fire. Some of the Regulars said today that in Menotomy a British bullet shot a pin from his wig."

I looked down at my plate. My face flushed.

"Was he hurt?" Mary asked.

"No," Paul assured her. "Not our Doctor Warren. I heard he was even going under fire to help the wounded."

"Dear man," Debby said sarcastically.

"Did we win?" Frances asked.

Paul bent over his soup bowl. "Not yet, my lamb," he said, "not yet. But we will."

"What happened to Lord Percy?" I asked.

Paul raised his eyes and looked at me. "He met Colonel Smith as they were coming back through Lexington. His brigade joined the fight. But he was taken aback to find so many men in the field against him."

"I hope they shot him," I said.

"Sarah!" Rachel scolded. "For shame."

"Did they, Paul?" I persisted.

"No. He reorganized the march. But more militia from surrounding counties kept coming. Some British at Province House were talking this afternoon, saying the town of Malden was sending small boys on horseback with saddle-bags full of food for the men. Other towns sent wagons of food. The British had nothing. Our militia pressed on, attacking and attacking and then . . ." Paul paused with a sense of drama akin to Father's.

"And then?" Mary asked.

"A tall man with long gray hair, on a white horse, kept appearing in fields and on hillocks. He'd get off the horse, lay his long musket on the saddle, and the horse would stand very still. Then he'd fire and hit a Regular, climb on his horse again, gallop off, and appear somewhere else."

"Who was he?" Frances fairly screamed.

Paul shook his head. "Nobody knows. Some old farmer. I heard the Regulars at Province House say they dreaded the sight of him." Paul looked at me. "To answer your question, Sarah. Percy made it safely back to Boston. Now lambs, go in the other room and play. Let me have my coffee in peace."

They scrambled off their chairs and left. Paul looked at us. He smiled sheepishly. "Thank you, Rachel," he said. "I always wanted a chance to be Father."

Chapter Eighteen

A LETTER CAME from Father, finally. It was brought to the house late Thursday night by Mr. Bowdoin.

We passed it from one to the other. Father called Rachel "my dear girl." He was in Cambridge, where the Committee of Safety was sitting. Doctor Warren was the chairman. Thousands of minutemen were pouring into Harvard Yard from the surrounding countryside. Doctor Warren was trying to organize and feed them.

As for himself, he was going to start riding express for the Committee. He needed money.

"I am in want of some clean linen and stockings very much," he wrote.

But he did not tell us how to get these things to him.

Doctor Church stood in our kitchen. "Enough writing, Mrs. Revere," he said. "I must be on my way."

"Drink your coffee, Doctor Church. I will be finished in a minute."

The rest of us sat around the table. All that could be heard was the *scratch-scratch-scratch* of Rachel's quill pen.

Paul stood over her, protectively. He never took his eyes from Church. Everything about Paul showed his dislike for the man who had appeared at our door so suddenly, accompanied by one of Gage's aides, who now waited outside.

It was Sunday. Church bells pealed. But we had other concerns than keeping the Sabbath this day. Doctor Church had told us Boston would soon be under siege by the Americans. No one would be able to get in or out. Any Whig leader who attempted to cross British lines was certain of hanging.

"How did *you* manage to get in, Doctor?" Paul asked him.

"I had a special pass. I've come for medicines. For both American and British officers. Even with that I was seized at Boston Neck, made a prisoner, and taken to Gage. They allowed me only one visit to my home and surgery. I must be out of town by noon."

"But they allowed you to come here?" Paul asked.

Church smiled. He was a tall, gaunt man. And he had about him some quality of complicity that I did not like. "Your father begged me to manage it. And even a major can be bribed. Are you finished yet, madam?"

Rachel signed the note with a flourish and handed it to Paul, who read it aloud to us.

"My dear. By Doctor Church I send a hundred and twenty-five pounds and beg you will take the best care of yourself and not attempt coming into this town again. And if I have an opportunity of coming or sending out anything or any of the children I shall do it. Pray, keep up your spirits and trust yourself and us in the hands of a good God, who will take care of us. 'Tis all my dependence, for vain is the help of man. Adieu, my love. From your affectionate Rachel."

"Very good, madam." Doctor Church held out his hand for the note. But Paul did not hand it over.

"Where will you get a hundred and twenty-five pounds?" he asked Rachel.

Rachel was already reaching for her cloak. "From the cash box at the shop," she said. "Come, Paul, you will accompany me there now, and bring the money to Doctor Church before he leaves town. We can't leave your father on the charity of friends."

Then she paused. "Doctor Church, you say you bribed the major to let you stop here."

"That I did, madam."

"Would you say then, that bribes work with many of Gage's aides?"

"For what purpose, madam?"

"For the purpose, Doctor, of getting us a pass out of this town. I sent Paul yesterday. None were available. You were at Province House this morning. What is the mood there?"

"Chaos, madam. There are few passes to be had. But for the lucky few who know the right people to listen to a tale of woe."

"Could you give us the name of one such person?" Rachel asked.

He thought for a moment. "There is Captain Irving," he said.

"Could you find out how much of a tale of woe it would take to move him?"

Church bowed. "You will receive a note from him this afternoon, madam," he said.

My brother's face was very white at this exchange. I did not understand. I would, later that day.

I STOOD in line in an anteroom of Province House. It was crowded, noisy, and hot. At the far end, a British officer sat behind a desk. A small placard in front of him read "Major Small." I knew him to be a friend of Doctor Warren's, mayhap the only officer in the British army on whom Warren looked fondly.

But I would not trade on that. Not if it killed me.

In a far corner was a pile of goods, guarded by a sentry. Baskets of eggs, a firkin of butter that would soon melt in the heat, even some chickens cackling in a cage. There were bottles of wine, shanks of ham wrapped in burlap, loaves of gingerbread, barrels of precious flour.

The people were bringing the bounty from their larders to bribe Gage's men for passes out of town.

It was what Rachel had meant by "how much of a tale of woe" would be needed to get us a pass out of town.

A note, suggesting how much woe, had been given to Paul by Doctor Church at Province House when Paul delivered the money to Church for Father.

"By desire of Capt. Irving," it said, "we are given to understand you have some veal and spirits to send over, which will be very acceptable. There is a pass ready for Mrs. Revere, family, and effects." It was signed by a Sergeant Singer.

In a basket I had two bottles of beer, one of wine, and a shank of veal. In my hand I had Singer's note.

I had not wanted to do it. "It's wrong," I told Rachel. "We need the food. You heard Church say soon there will be only salt pork and dried fish left in town."

"We will be gone by then," she said.

"Suppose they aren't good for their word?"

"They will be. Gage's men are already hungry. It will turn the trick for us."

"Send Debby, then."

"She's gone to Doctor Eustis to get medicines for your grandmother. Paul is at your father's shop. You must go."

So I stood in line, the basket heavy on my arm, anger growing inside me. Ahead of me were at least a dozen people, women with crying babies, old men, and youngsters sent on like missions by their parents. The line wound down the street. The open windows only let in the stultifying heat and the flies.

When the person up front got to Major Small, his assistant would check their offering against the letter they held and have a clerk set the food aside. Then Major Small would give them a pass.

I felt anger. Boston's larders were daily getting empty. People were hungry. And these arrogant, red-coated devils were using their authority to squeeze the last loaf of bread out of the citizens, for a promise of safe passage.

Behind me someone echoed my thoughts. "The blackguards. Might as well hold a pistol to your head."

"It's worth it if it gets us out of town. Didn't you hear? Benjamin Edes, printer of the *Gazette,* got out. But they've put his nineteen-year-old son in prison."

Then from someone else, a furtive whisper. "Who says where we're going is any better? I heard that four thousand of our militiamen were killed."

"Rumor," from still another. "They're saying that at Jonas Clarke's meetinghouse in Lexington, soldiers killed three at worship. And a woman, who'd lain but a few days after giving birth, was stabbed by British in Concord. But it's all rumor."

The whispers grew around me. Rumors like this were flying like bullets through town. I wished I could cover my ears. Then, of a sudden, measured footsteps sounded on the wide floorboards, and I became sensible of an officer standing over me.

"Ah, Miss Sarah. We meet again." He bowed.

Lord Percy! He was smiling down at me.

"Miss Sarah Revere." He murmured my name again. Then he looked to see who was watching and perceiving that no one was, moved closer. "What have you in the basket?" He lifted the white napkin, inspected the basket's contents, tossed the edge of the napkin back, and looked at me. "Do you think this is enough to make up for the loss of thirty-six of my fusiliers and seventy Royal Marines the other day?" he whispered.

I thought the man mad. "It isn't my intention to make up for your losses, sir. I'm sure no one can do that."

"What is your intention, then?"

"To secure a pass for my family."

He laughed. "Let me have the basket, Miss Sarah." He reached out a slender hand.

I clasped it tight and close to me. "I'm instructed to hand over the contents to no one but Captain Irving."

"Indeed."

"Yes."

"You will hand it over to me, Sarah Revere. And now."

"I will not." My face flamed. I stepped back from him.

This whole exchange took only a minute. And there was such a babble of voices in the room that people took scant notice.

Percy smiled at me. But it was more a leer.

"May I remind you that as a colonel I outrank Captain Irving?"

I held fast to my basket. Surely he could not expect to get away with this. Surely, even in the chaos that now existed in Boston, even in the new order of things, there was still some honor left.

But I knew there wasn't. And I knew that if I handed my bribes over to this unscrupulous man, our chance of ever getting a pass out of town was doomed.

Once again he looked about to see who was watching. No one was. "Either hand the basket over, Miss Sarah," he hissed, "or forfeit your place in line."

In one blind instant I wanted to hit him with it. And in that instant he came to represent to me all the power, arrogance, and disdain of the king's men who had taken over our town.

I felt a great surge of self-pity inside me. But it was soon diminished by anger. I did not know what I would do. But I would not hand the contents of my basket over to this fop of a man, who took such pleasure in bullying a woman.

I stepped out of line.

For a moment I stood there and glared at him.

"If your actions today, sir, are an example of the way you and your kind treat ordinary people, I would say it is fortunate for us all that you lost thirty-six fusiliers and seventy Royal Marines the other day."

Then I ran from the room out into the sunlight.

MY WORDS filled me with triumph, but only for a few minutes. Out in the crowded street, I stood stock-still. What to do now? I could not go home. Rachel was packing. She expected me to come with a pass. She was planning to leave within a week.

No, I could not go home.

I looked around me. The streets were filled with people who all seemed to be hurrying somewhere with a great sense of purpose. I noticed many wagons filled with household goods. Families were leaving. How could so many people be leaving of a sudden? Where had they all gotten their passes?

I hurried forward, pushing against the crowd. *I should have spoken up,* I pondered. I should have asked for Captain Irving. I should have stood my ground and yelled and screamed.

How could I be so stupid?

"*Psst,* girl. 'Ave you any vittles in the basket?"

I did not realize he was speaking to me at first. I was so intent on my misery and wondering what I would tell Rachel about my blunder. I had just about decided that the only thing to do was to go to Mr. Bowdoin when I felt a slight touch on my arm.

"Girl. I say 'ave you any food in the basket?"

I looked up into the thin, drawn face of a chimney sweep. I recognized him from our neighborhood, though not by name.

"No."

"Me mum is sickly to home. I saw you comin' out of Province House carryin' the basket ever so careful-like. And not swingin' it like it wuz empty. I figure they turned you down for a pass. Am I right?"

The cheek! "What business is it of yours?"

"Could be my business, if you want. Could be you'd trade me that food for a pass out of town."

"Where would *you* get a pass?"

He reached inside his dirty coat and drew out some chits.

Passes. Several of them. Signed by Gage.

I gasped. "Where did you get those?"

"Hush. I cleaned the chimneys at Province House. Had to go inside to do this. These passes were just sittin' there on a desk. And the room wuz empty."

I stared at him in disbelief.

"Like I say, me mum is sickly to home. And I can't buy enough food with my paltry earnings. There's little to be had. So I got to thinkin', what's the difference if I give out the passes or they do? You see any difference?"

The innocence in his blue eyes was real. His somberness, his plight, touched me. "No," I said, "I see no difference."

"Me mum needs the food more than those fat slobs. So I stand here. And I wait for the people who come out with full baskets. Means they've been refused passes. And they're spirited up in anger enough to trade."

I nodded my head vigorously.

"So, miss, you wanna trade some food for a pass?"

"Yes," I said. And I handed over the basket. No, he didn't want the basket. He'd just take the food, he said. And he did. He took the veal and the wine and the beer, opened his ragged coat, and stuffed it all into deep pockets.

"Me mum sewed them inside me coat," he said.

"Why don't you take one of those passes and get out of town?" I asked him.

He shook his head. "Me mum is better off here. And besides, I've got more chimneys to clean."

"Thank you," I murmured. I smiled at him. Then I hugged him around the middle.

"Here, miss, why would you do a thing like that?"

"To thank you proper."

" 'Tis a fair trade we made."

"To thank you for more than that," I said. "You don't know what you are, do you?"

"I'm a chimney sweep, miss."

"No. You're more than that. You are one of us. The common people. Against the king. You've outfoxed all those smart British officers in there. You're what the common folk are. Don't make little of yourself. Please."

And having said such, I ran home.

Chapter Nineteen

*P*AUL, WHERE DID you get the pistol?"

It was hard leaving. For about the sixth time, Rachel went running back into the house for something. For some reason, I followed.

It was terrible leaving. Especially since we could take only so many personal things. Only so much could fit in the cart. And it also had to carry Grandmother, who still had a sickness in her bones, as well as household goods.

"Paul!" Rachel stood in the sun-washed doorway. I stood just behind her.

My brother had just taken a pistol from a concealed place in the hearth, which was cold and black on this May morning, already an ash pit of memory.

"It's all right, Rachel, don't worry the matter."

She went into the kitchen. The house had an unlived-in look, as if abandoned. I couldn't bear going inside again, but I did.

"Where did you get it?" Rachel stood, hands on hips.

"I have friends."

"From your father's uncle Thomas, I suppose. The old fool. No wonder his son Benjamin was arrested for unlawful acts against the king. Do you want to end up on that prison ship in the harbor? Like Benjamin?"

Paul was stuffing the pistol inside his coat. "I'll not end up on any prison ship. Benjamin was stupid, refusing to turn in his musket."

"And what of you and this pistol, then?"

"Nobody knows I've got it. Rachel, there's no telling what those sentries will do on the Neck. I'm going along to protect you and the children. What means do I have, if not this pistol?"

Rachel stepped forward. "Give it to me, Paul. Or don't come with us. You must promise not to take it out unless they come into this house and attack you."

Paul put the pistol back in the hiding place in the hearth.

"I don't know if it's a good plan, having you sup with your father's uncle Thomas while we're gone," Rachel said. "The man fills your head with ideas."

Paul laughed. "Don't worry about me, Rachel. I'll keep."

Paul was not coming with us. Father had written that he should stay. Paul was a man now, and would look out for Father's house and shop. We went outside, and he locked the house.

"Are you coming?" Rachel asked Debby.

My sister glared at her, sour as bad milk. She was huddled in a far corner of the yard with Amos Lincoln, who was staying. They'd been kissing, I could tell. Mayhap doing more.

"Why can't I stay?" Debby whined for the hundreth time that morning. "I'm older than Paul."

"Then act it," Rachel snapped. "I need you. And your father wants you. Now come along, Debby, I mean it."

Paul took Militia's reins to lead her out of the yard.

Debby came, dragging her feet.

"Keep that gingerbread well hidden," Rachel told her. "It's all we have to sustain us until we get there."

The British would not allow anyone to take food out of the city. But Rachel had smuggled some ham and some sugar in a featherbed.

Debby hid the precious loaf under some hay in the cart.

"Elizabeth, get in the cart," Rachel ordered.

"Wanna walk."

"In the cart! Now!"

Elizabeth scrambled in. Ruffles jumped in with her.

"Frances, you too. With all those clothes you've got on, you'll never make it, child."

Frances was wearing at least four petticoats, two short gowns, her go-to-meeting cloak, and two pair of hose. And the day was warm.

We started off, a strange procession, but no stranger than any other that fair May day. The streets were crowded with families such as ours. All had carts or wagons overflowing with household goods. We passed houses that had been abandoned as people left. Houses that stood with vacant-eyed windows, and doors open. In one a chicken was standing in the front hall.

We wound down Fish Street, then Ann Street, through Dock Square, and onto Marlborough, which turned into Newbury.

On Orange Street, Grandmother sat up. "It's time for my tea," she said.

She had not spoken much all through her illness. Half the time she had been feverish.

"Soon as we get through the town gates," Rachel promised.

"The town gates?" Grandmother looked around. Then she fell back asleep. "Wake me," she said.

As it turned out, we did not have to wake her. She knew when we reached that stretch of salt marshes and scrub, with the Charles River on our left and the Mystic on our right, where we were. We were on the Neck.

The Neck was where Mark was. The subject of one of her favorite stories. She sat up again. "Mark. Children, look, there he is." And she pointed a bony finger.

There, indeed, was Mark, up ahead. Or all that was left of the slave hung in chains years ago for helping Phyllis murder their master. The iron chains still swung in the breezes that came off the water. We walked right under it. You could scarce make out the old gathering of bones as a self-respecting skeleton. But Grandmother recognized it.

"There, children, there is Mark. Let his bones be a lesson to you."

"Stop it," Debby said. "You're frightening them."

But the children were laughing. Nothing frightened them today. They were on a lark. They were on their way to see Father.

"I want my tea now," Grandmother demanded.

Debby produced it. Rachel had brought it in a covered stone jar. Rachel poured some into a mug for Grandmother, who sat up drinking it and smacking her lips as she did so.

ABOUT THE time that we got to the sentry posts on the Neck, we noticed a swarm of carts and wagons coming toward us.

"Tories," Paul said, "coming back into Boston for protection."

"Some protection they'll get," Rachel murmured. "Do they know there is little to eat in town but salt meat and fish?"

The narrow stretch of road could scarcely accommodate traffic going both ways. And ofttimes wagons of Tory families coming in were scraped and bumped against those of Patriot families going out.

"Mother Revere, make sure you sit firm on that featherbed where I've stuffed the ham and sugar," Rachel whispered.

"They'll not move me, the rascals," Grandmother said. "And I feel pity for any soldier who tries."

When our turn came to be inspected, the sergeant approached our wagon with a bayonet fixed on the end of his musket.

"Move over, old woman," he directed Grandmother.

"Hey? I'm sickly. Can't you see? I'll not move for you. Or your king."

"Move, I say." And he made as if to raise his bayonet at her.

In an instant, Ruffles sprang forward, a deep growl in his throat.

"Hold back the dog," the sentry ordered. "Hold him back, I say, or I'll run him through."

I saw my brother step forward. And saw Rachel's hand on his arm. "Let Grandmother take care of herself, Paul," she whispered, "or she'll never forgive you."

How clever of Rachel!

Paul lifted Ruffles out of the cart. Then stepped away.

Grandmother sat up, all thought of sick bones forgotten. She pushed the musket aside. "Do you want to stab me, young man? Would that profit your day?"

The sergeant did not know what to do.

"Go ahead," Grandmother directed, "stab me." She was spoiling for a fight.

The sergeant flushed. "I'll not harm an old woman," he mumbled, "but I've got to inspect your cart."

And with that he went around Grandmother, jabbing the bayonet into the hay.

He came up with the loaf of gingerbread on the end of it.

"What's this?"

"What does it look like?" Grandmother asked.

"No food allowed out of Boston. By orders of Gage."

"It's for the children," Grandmother said.

The sergeant unwrapped the towel from the gingerbread, smelled it, and raised his eyes heavenward. "By God," he said, "it's too good for Rebel children." And he took it away.

I thought Grandmother would die from apoplexy on the spot. She made as if to raise herself up. "You had better be damned for taking bread from children!"

There was no accounting for what would have happened to her and to us if a clear, firm voice from an oncoming carriage hadn't interrupted. "Is that any way to treat an elderly woman? Haven't you any respect?"

"Dear God," I heard Rachel murmur.

"The Queen herself," from Debby, whose mood remained foul.

I was the last to see who it was. There seemed to be a commotion up ahead. A woman jumped down from the elegant carriage, the top of which was piled with trunks and goods. I later counted three beds, piles of bedding, six trunks, a chest, some small kegs, some hay, three bags of corn, and two small pigs. At least three Tory officers on horseback accompanied her.

Lady Frankland.

"You there," she shouted to the sergeant. "You make me ashamed of being under the Crown. Shall I turn my carriage around this day and throw my lot in with the Rebels, then?"

"Lady Frankland." The officer in charge came

out from behind his sentry post to greet her. "Don't bother yourself with this rabble. Get back in your carriage."

"I happen to know this rabble, sir." She stood in the dusty road, wrapped in yards and yards of silk and flounces. "These people are friends of mine. And I say give them back their gingerbread, or I'll not move from this spot."

The officer in charge, harassed and tired and hot, took off his tricorn and wiped his brow. "Lady Frankland, surely this is no concern of yours."

"It is every bit my concern when soldiers of the king harass old women and children. And take from them their last bit of food. Give it back, I say, or I shall stand here all day and block the road with my carriage."

The officer conferred with those who accompanied Lady Frankland, then turned to the sergeant. "Sergeant, return the gingerbread," he said.

The sergeant obeyed, reluctantly.

"That's more to my liking," Lady Frankland said. Then she ordered her driver to fetch one of the bags of corn and give it to us.

He did so. Lady Frankland did not move until

he set it in the cart. All this while, Rachel stood there stock-still. As did Paul and I. Grandmother was sitting up, her mouth open.

"Lady Frankland, Lady Frankland," the children screamed and ran to her. She hugged them. She reached into the fancy pocket she wore around her waist and drew out some maple sugar candy and gave it to them. Then she sent them back to the cart and turned to Rachel. All the while her British sentries stood guard with drawn pistols.

She and Rachel embraced. "My heart tears asunder, seeing all this," Lady Frankland said. "What have we wrought? We are, in part, responsible, you and I, Rachel. Are you sorry?"

"No," Rachel said. "We did what was right to do. But I fear for Margaret."

Margaret who? I did not understand. *What had they done? How could they be responsible?* The thought nagged me, but I put it aside. There was too much in front of my mind.

Lady Frankland hugged Rachel again. "I have been honored to know you," she said. "I shall miss you and await your return to Boston."

Rachel, near tears now for the first time this day, only nodded.

Now Grandmother spoke. "Lady Frankland."

She turned. "Hello, Mother Revere."

Grandmother pulled herself up and leaned on the side of the cart. "Come here," she said.

For only an instant, Lady Frankland hesitated. Grandmother had never said a word to her. At least not a good word. But she walked to the side of the cart nevertheless.

"Yes, Mrs. Revere?"

"Thank you," Grandmother said.

"I was honored to help."

"You'll bring their wrath down upon you when you return to Boston," Grandmother said.

Lady Frankland laughed. "I have no fear, Mother Revere. I lost all my fear twenty years ago in Portugal, when we had the earthquake. And I ran through the streets afterward looking for my Henry. And dug him out of the rubble, where he was near buried alive, with my own hands."

Grandmother said no more. She was spent. The whole proceeding had exhausted her. Debby stepped forward to settle her in the wagon again. But she said nothing to Lady Frankland. She did not even acknowledge her.

I could see that Lady Frankland was hurt by

Debby's snub. It was a terrible thing to do when the woman had just rescued us from such a plight.

I watched Lady Frankland walk back to her carriage. And I felt something pulling at me, pulling and pushing at the same time.

I knew what I must do. I must make up for the rudeness of my sister Debby. Rachel could not do it, nor could Paul. It fell to me.

"Lady Frankland!" I called out.

She stopped and turned.

I rushed forward, past the sergeant, who was glowering at me. He reached out and grabbed my arm. "Let me go!" I demanded. But he held me firm.

"Unhand her, sergeant," his officer ordered.

The brute did so. And I ran forward past Lady Frankland's sentries to put my arms around her. "We'll miss you, too," I said.

"Dear Sarah." She touched my face. "You've become such a lovely young lady. It seems like only yesterday I was your age. Grow well, Sarah, and do not give your heart to just anybody."

What did she mean? I dared not think. I gave her one more hug, then turned and ran back to the wagon.

Then we had to say good-bye to Paul. There wasn't much time. The men at the sentry post were hard put for patience. Good-byes were quick. Paul hugged each of us, then turned to walk back.

"Come along, Paul," Lady Frankland offered.

I turned to see my brother stand stock-still and hesitate. I knew what he was thinking. Ride with a Tory? Or with a friend?

Then he smiled and ran to jump in her carriage.

Rachel sighed deeply. "He'll be all right," she said. "He knows how to think for himself. He knows how to behave. He'll do us proud."

And so we moved on ahead, to make the seven miles up the Charles to Watertown.

Margaret? Margaret who? I pondered. And then, before we'd gone two miles it came to me.

Margaret Gage.

Watertown

Chapter Twenty

17 • JUNE • 1775

*W*HAT HAVE I been thinking? Did I fall asleep? Was I dreaming of being back in Boston? Why, it must be one o'clock by now. Father will stop his printing of money and be looking for his noon meal. Where is Rachel? Still sleeping?

Oh, the day is hot. The sun is climbing in the heavens. And the cannon! Oh, I wish I could muffle my ears!

I went into the house. All was quiet. I went into the kitchen, took some cold meat and cheese and beer, gathered it on a tray. Enough for John Cook and Father. I walked through the house to the shop.

Father looked up from his workbench. "Has Warren come by yet?"

"No. But you should eat. Where's John?"

"Gone on an errand for me."

"You mean he's not here?"

"What words have I just spoken, Sarah? Are you all right, girl? Or are you ailing?"

"I fell asleep in the arbor."

"With those guns sounding like that? Did the reverend go?"

"Yes."

"Good. Ah, this is a lovely repast. You are becoming a real boon to me, Sarah. Come sit with me a while."

"Father, now that John's gone, I would ask you a question."

"Where's Rachel?"

"Sleeping. Father?"

"Ask away." He was chewing happily.

"Do you know who fired the first shot at Lexington?"

He stopped chewing. All was silent in the shop. Even the distant cannon had quieted for the moment. "I thought we had all that settled, Sarah."

"No, it isn't settled."

"Did the reverend ask you this, then?"

"Yes."

"What did you tell him?"

"What you told me to tell him."

He looked down at his food. "I see. And now you would ask me what really happened."

"Yes."

"Isn't it terrible enough that I know, Sarah?"

"Then it *was* the Americans."

"I didn't say that."

"But you said . . ."

"I said isn't it terrible enough that I know?"

"But what mean you by that, Father?"

He sipped his mug of beer. "Think on it, Sarah. No one else knows. Just knowing is terrible, no matter who it was. Sarah, believe this."

I nodded. I was holding my breath and I let it out slowly. I was trying to understand. "What meaning am I to take from this, Father? That you will never tell anyone?"

"That's the only meaning I can give it, Sarah." He said this so sadly.

"Why?"

"There's no profit in the telling, child."

"But how can you live with the knowing?"

"I must."

"People will always think you know, Father. They will always speculate."

"They have that right."

"It will follow, then, that it was the Americans. Or you would tell."

He said naught.

"Am I wrong, Father?"

"What do we so often speak of, Sarah? That what matters is not what people think, but what's true."

Oh, he plagued me so. "But what *is* true?" I was near to tears.

He put a hand out and touched my arm. "I shouldn't have let that reverend question you so. He's made you distraught."

"It isn't him. It's you. Why won't you tell me?"

"Sarah, Sarah, be calm. Be still. And hear me now. We all must decide, in our hearts, what's true. We must make our own truth every day. And hold it close. And not let anyone take it from us."

I said nothing. The sound of his voice soothed me. I needed to hear that voice. It made everything all right again. Though I feared things would never be all right again.

"It doesn't matter who fired that shot. It was fired. The British want to think it was us. We wish to blame them. What does it matter? We've both been moving toward it for years. But hear me, Sarah. Will you?"

I nodded.

"If we keep what we know as truth in our hearts, it will keep us strong. And bring us through. If we let people take it from us, we are nothing. So get your truths in order, Sarah. Run around and scramble and collect them. Pick them up from where they fall. Gather them in, as I've seen you do with your cotton threads when little Elizabeth pulls them away from you and tangles them all about on the floor."

I said, yes, I would.

"Now give me that pretty smile."

I smiled for him.

"What are you stitching now?"

"A new shirt for you."

"Good. I need one. And money is in short supply. Whatever do you suppose happened to that money Rachel gave to Doctor Church for me?"

"I don't know."

He sighed. "He told me Gage took it and the

note from him. I never liked the man, but I have made myself arrive at a truth about Church. I have decided to believe him. We all have, on the Committee. We can't waste time mistrusting each other. We must make our truths and move on. Or we will never have any peace in our hearts. Do you see what I am trying to tell you?"

"Yes."

He drew me close. He put his hand on the back of my neck and drew me to him. I was standing and he was perched on a stool, but I was at eye level with him.

He smiled. But only with his mouth. His eyes were not smiling when he looked into mine.

In those eyes, I saw the truth. I saw my father's secret.

It was there in his eyes for me to see, the truth reflected, as the trees and bushes and houses are reflected in the calm surface of water on a clear day.

And in that moment I knew there was only one truth. And not the truth as we make it for ourselves every day. *That* truth, the one we must make and live with, gets us through, yes. He was right. It may even give us some peace.

But only because we refuse to face the real truth of things when they are presented to us.

The real truth is clear, if we choose to see it. But it is also terrifying.

I hope I do not see it too often in life. I do not like it.

But in that moment, when our eyes held, I saw it in my father's eyes. He was giving it to me. And I took it.

I kissed him and turned to go.

"Let me know when Doctor Warren comes," he said.

"Yes, Father."

But my mind was not on my answer. *Now I know,* was all I could think. I was dizzy with the possibility of it. *Now I know who fired the first shot. And now I shall have to take the secret of it with me to the grave.*

Chapter Twenty-one

*S*o, WHAT GOOD was knowing, then? No good. No profit in it. The truth does not make one at peace. The truth hurts.

I walked, as one blinded, into the house with Father's empty dish. Then I heard Rachel coming down the stairs.

"My, I've had a good sleep. I feel refreshed. But oh, those cannon. Will they never stop?"

She came into the kitchen. "The others haven't returned yet?"

"No." I turned to her.

"What is it, Sarah?"

"Rachel, I have news."

Her hand went to her bosom. She sat down on a spindle-back chair. "Has Doctor Warren been around? Has he gone to the hill?"

"No, this is not about Warren."

"About what, then?"

"Let me get you some coffee. And some corn bread. There's some left from breakfast." I bustled about, preparing her repast. She watched my every move. I got a mug of coffee for myself, too, and sat across the long oak table from her.

"A reverend was here, Rachel. A Reverend William Gordon from Roxbury. Asking questions about Lexington."

She nodded. "I was expecting him. I met Benjamin Edes's wife in town this morning. She said he'd been by their house, too. What news did he bring?"

"He said General Gage booked passage for his wife on the *Charming Nancy*. He said Gage is sending her back to England."

Her face fell. She set her cup down gently. "Oh," she said. "Did he say why?"

"Yes. He said Gage suspected Margaret of being an informer. Of telling Doctor Warren in April that Gage was sending troops after the military stores at Concord."

"Oh," she said again.

"Rachel"—I leaned forward—"did she?"

"How would I know, Sarah?" She fastened her gaze on me, wide and innocent. "What brings you to think I know of this?"

"May I speak free?"

"Of course."

"I mind the night Warren supped with us. It was the first of June, last year. The Port of Boston had just been closed."

"A long time ago now." She sighed.

"Yes. But you pleaded with Doctor Warren to see Mrs. Gage, because she was afflicted with headaches. You said Lady Frankland begged you to ask."

"I disremember that, Sarah."

"Please, Rachel, try to recollect. Doctor Warren did not want to see her at first. But you told him she would be very discreet. Then he agreed."

"Yes." She smiled. "I remember. But what has that to do with anything?"

"Rachel, you and Lady Frankland sent Mrs. Gage to Doctor Warren."

"For her headaches," she said.

I felt something fall inside me in that place

inside us where things fall when we are disappointed. "You didn't send her to make an acquaintance with Warren? The headaches weren't a pretense?"

She'd gotten up and walked to a cupboard for another piece of corn bread. "This is very good."

"Lucy Knox made it."

"She's a dear, don't you think? And they're so in love."

"He's gone to the hill. He may be killed this day."

"Sarah." She whirled on me. "I don't know what it is that you are trying to say. But I know nothing about Margaret Gage being an informer. And if you thought I did, it would not be seemly for you to ask."

"Not seemly?"

"No."

"Why?"

"Because things were done that had to be done, Sarah. By so many of us. Things we choose not to speak of again."

"Is that what Lady Frankland meant when we met her coming out of Boston last month? When she said you and she were responsible? And asked you if you were sorry?"

"Who knows what Lady Frankland meant? She was so agitated that day. So was I. It was the heat of the moment. People say things, Sarah, in the heat of the moment."

"Rachel, you can tell me. Please."

"Why must you know?"

We faced one another. And I could not speak. *Because,* I told myself, *if this is what was between you and Warren, I have made a terrible mistake. I accused him of having feelings for you that he should not have. And I need to know now if this is what was between you. And not the other. I need to know before he goes to the hill.*

But I could not say the words aloud to her. I would die first.

"Sarah," she said, and came over and put her hand on my head. "Don't ask any more questions. I don't mind for myself. But what of Doctor Warren?"

I looked up at her.

"Whomever his informer was, he has gone out of his way not to divulge it. He wishes the identity to be known to him alone. He wishes to take the secret with him to the grave."

More secrets taken to the grave this day. I could not bear it. I got up.

"We must give him that, Sarah. Don't you think?"

I nodded, yes. Of course she was right. But in giving him that, was I protecting another secret they had together?

Must I give him that, too?

Then I thought of what Father had said before. That he'd decided to believe Doctor Church. That we can't waste time mistrusting one another. That we must make our truths and move on. Or we will never have any peace in our hearts.

I looked at Rachel again. She was smiling at me serenely. Whatever she'd done, whatever she knew, she had peace in her heart.

She's always been good to me, I minded. She's kept our family together. She made us a family again, when we were falling apart. Father is happy with her. Why do I keep gnawing at this thing, like a dog with an old bone?

"Rachel, may I ask you another question?"

"Of course."

"You hold Doctor Warren in high esteem, don't you?"

She laughed. "I think he's a fool for wanting to fight today."

"But you care for him." I eyed her cautiously.

"Of course," she said simply. "I love him, Sarah."

"You *love* him?"

"Yes. Your father and I both love him. He's become very dear to me. As a friend."

"A friend?"

"Yes. Why do you ask?"

"Is it seemly to say such about a man, Rachel?" I whispered.

She laughed. "Of course."

"You mean it isn't improper?"

"I know what's in my heart, Sarah. I love your father. But I can love Doctor Warren, too, can't I? As a friend? There's enough room in my heart for that, I would hope."

"Is there?"

"Yes." Then she frowned. "There are different kinds of love, Sarah. I feel one kind of love for your father. A special kind. Another kind for Warren. And still a different kind for you children." She smiled at me. "Heaven rue the day we can't feel love for one another. I wouldn't want to live in such a world, would you?"

I shook my head, numbly. "No."

"Sarah, I know not what afflicts you, but I

wager it has to do with Warren. Your father and I are not blind. We know you two have had some quarrel. You should set it right. It's festering inside you."

I said nothing.

"Warren senses it. Many times, of late, you've been rude to him. He is much hurt by it. He doesn't deserve such. He is a dear and true friend."

"He's changed," I said.

"You're growing up, becoming a woman. Mayhap you're seeing him in a different light now, and not with the eyes of a child any longer. This is to be expected. But keep in mind. He hasn't changed. You have. He is fixed in his feelings for you. Settle this thing between you, if you have a chance. It is not good to let things fester."

I nodded, taking in her words.

"Now I must go and see to baby Joshua. He should be waking."

She went into the center hall. I heard her footsteps on the floorboards. Then her exclamation. "Oh, speaking of the devil, here he is now. Come in, Joseph, come in."

Chapter Twenty-two

*S*ETTLE IT, INDEED. I stood in the kitchen, watching her open the front door. He came in. He had his man with him, his nigra servant, Damien.

She was so good of heart. And trusting, I minded. Clever, but too trusting. She did not know that this thing that lay between me and Warren was about her.

She did not know that he had admitted to me that he found her pretty and interesting and smart, that he was a man and not made of stone.

Would she be greeting him so lightly now, if she knew?

I stood watching them in the hall. Sunlight, dappled by trees just outside, flickered on their forms.

He was wearing his best. His butter-colored frock coat, his wig tied back in a queue with a bit of black ribbon. His silk waistcoat. There was a sprig of green stuck in the buttonhole of his frock coat.

He was dressed as for a frolic.

"I'm going," I heard him tell Rachel.

"Why?" she asked.

"I've a mind to go."

"You're not fit. Last night you drank yourself into oblivion. You can't hold your wine, Joseph. And you're not dressed for command."

"I've slept. I was up at first light. Went to Hastings House in Cambridge. Elbridge Gerry and I talked the matter over."

"And? What did Elbridge Gerry advise?"

"We agreed that occupying Charlestown was the utmost folly. He decided it would be foolish to put myself in danger. Then we both agreed that if I must go, I must go. Prescott offered me the command, but I go as a private soldier."

"Men." She stood very close to him. In her hand she held the corner of her apron. She was no coquette, Rachel. She wasn't using her feminine wiles. No one I knew had less feminine wiles than she.

"I wish you wouldn't," she told him. "I shall be put out with you, if you die."

"Nor do I wish to die."

"That isn't what you said last night."

"It was the wine talking last night."

"And what is talking today, then?"

"The need in me to be with those who are out there. Finishing what I started."

"You were not alone in starting it."

"But I assembled this army. They came in answer to my circulars. I spirited them up."

She sighed.

"The British have landed and engaged. I must go to the men. Colonel Prescott is there. But I must be, too."

"Very well. But have a care, Joseph."

"Yes. I will."

They stood, inches apart, looking at one another. His hands were clasped behind his back.

I waited and watched.

"Paul wants to see you before you go," she said. "He is in the shop."

He nodded. "You understand, Rachel. I can't ask those men to do what I am not willing to do myself."

"No, Joseph. I do not understand. But I respect your feelings. You have always been an honorable man. Perhaps only *I* know how honorable. I could not care for you otherwise."

She was telling him. She was letting him know she knew he cared for her. And that he had always been honorable. She was giving him this, as a gift, to take with him to the hill.

He knew it. He took a step forward and embraced her. It was quick and passionless. Yet full of feeling. Then he walked out the door and gestured to Damien, who followed him around to the back entrance of the shop.

"Have a care, Joseph," she said. And she stood there, looking after him for a moment. Then she turned and saw me watching. "Oh, Sarah," she said, "the fool man is going off to get himself killed."

I said nothing.

"I—" And she burst into tears then. "Oh, forgive me. I must see to Joshua."

The baby was crying. She ran upstairs.

I STOOD there waiting. My head was pounding from the sound of the cannon. I felt sick. *I must do something*, I decided. *Now.*

But what?

I must talk to him. No, I must give him something. No, I must talk to him first. Then give him something. Something to take with him. Like Rachel had done. To make up for everything.

Food, I thought. *He'll need food.* Then I ran to a window in the parlor, looked out, and saw Damien standing in the back yard. He had two sacks with him. *Food*, I thought. *And medical supplies.*

And then, of a sudden, it came to me what I would give him. I ran upstairs to the small room I occupied on the second floor. From a table I picked up the book he had commented on that dreadful night I had fought with him. *The Love Sonnets of William Shakespeare.*

I ran back downstairs with it. Then I hesitated. Would he think me foolish? A silly, lovestruck girl? He was going off to fight. To be with the army he had brought into being. No, I couldn't give him a book of poetry.

As I was standing there, addled as the town idiot, I caught sight of him through the parlor windows.

He was leaving.

He had said good-bye to Father. He was talking with Damien. They were coming round to the front of the house again. They were on the front walk. They were walking away.

I ran through the center hall and threw open the door.

"Doctor Warren!"

He turned. "Hello, Sarah."

I stood there, mute.

"What is it?"

I stepped out into the terrible heat, onto the front step. "I would speak with you."

He looked distracted. He murmured something to Damien, who nodded and went down the walk, opened the gate, and waited a distance away, under a tree. He nodded at me.

I went down the walk toward him.

"Yes, Sarah?" His voice was cold. My spirits fell. There was a distance between us.

Just then there came a fresh sounding of

cannon. He turned in the direction of the boom-
ing sound. He took his pocket watch out and
consulted it. "Yes, Sarah," he said again.

"I would see you before you go."

He made an attempt at a smile. But it was
shallow. "Forgive me, child. I'm in a rush. And
I've the devil's own headache this day. I slept
too late. I should be there on the hill now. They
need me."

It was too late.

It was as I'd thought. The time for settling it
had come and gone. We only get so many
chances to make things right with another human
being. And then the time is passed from us.

I looked up into his handsome face. He was
not here, I minded. He was here in body, but in
his heart and mind, he was already on the hill.

He was already gone from us.

"Doctor Warren, I would make things right
between us."

Another boom of cannon. This time louder.

"Damien," he called, "start off. I'll be along
in a minute."

The man waved and went.

"You were saying, Sarah?"

"I would make things right between us."

He scowled and shook his head. "No matter, Sarah," he said.

"Yes, it does matter. It matters dreadfully to me. I've been vile to you. I said shameful things. I would make them right."

He was shaking his head, no, no. He took a step away. He wanted to leave. I was besetting him.

He looked at me again and smiled. It was not a real smile. It did not go to his eyes. "We'll talk, Sarah. Soon."

"Now!"

"I can't." Another boom of the cannon. "I must go, child." People were coming out of their houses on the street.

"I'm not a child, Doctor Warren!"

"Dear God," he murmured. Then he looked at me fully for the first time. "Look, Sarah, it's all too late for this."

"That's what you said to me when you left Boston."

"I was anxious to be off then. As I am now."

"I was vile to you in Boston, too, blaming you for leaving, telling you Mr. Bowdoin was staying and blaming you because you weren't. Doctor Warren, you must forgive me!"

My words were drowned out by the cannon. My lips formed the words, but he could not hear them. The cannon were increasing in intensity now. *He hadn't heard me.*

He put a hand on my shoulder. "Be of good heart, Sarah. I must go."

"Take this. Please."

He'd turned to leave and stopped. "What is it?"

I gave him the book of poetry.

He looked at it and scowled. Did he not recognize it?

"It's the one you said you wanted to read. That night when you came to my room to tend to me when I was sick. The night we quarreled," I said lamely.

He smiled and nodded. "Thank you, Sarah." Then he put the book of Shakespeare in a pocket inside his frock coat. "Thank you," he said again.

And he started down the walk. At the gate he turned and waved. And he said something.

I think it was "I forgive you, Sarah," but I couldn't be certain because the cannon boomed again. I only saw his lips forming the words, but I could not hear them.

Chapter Twenty-three

*H*E NEVER CAME BACK. He died on the hill. Up to his knees in blood.

We waited. Rumors flew about town all day. We were winning, we were losing. The Americans ran out of powder.

None of it was true and all of it was true.

In the sweet June dusk, as the heat was abating and the sound of the cannon ceased, Damien came to the front door.

"Oh, please," he said to Rachel and my father, "they done kilt my master."

But even Damien didn't know for sure.

Warren had sent him off the hill. He, too, had only heard rumor.

But it was true.

Because next the Tory doctor Jeffries came, dusty and with blood on him. It was he Warren suggested should see Mrs. Gage for her headaches. Warren was dead, Jeffries said. He had seen the body. He looked at my father earnestly.

"Captain Walter Laurie, who'd led the British at North Bridge the day of the fighting at Concord, buried him. Laurie said, 'I stuffed the scoundrel with another Rebel into one hole. And there he and his seditious principles may remain.' " Jeffries spoke in low tones. "It made me ashamed to be one of them."

It was not a time to be dead. It was a time to come walking through the front gate in the sweet June dusk. It was a time to recite poetry. Even Debby cried.

"He was standing in the thick of it," Jeffries said, "and Major Small was there. He was one British officer who always liked Warren. He called out to Warren, 'For God's sake, stop. And please surrender.' Warren turned his head to acknowledge the call of his one friend in the British army. Told him he'd never surrender. And was shot."

Rachel was crying. I heard Father clear his throat. "He was thirty-four years old," he said.

Jeffries went on. "Here's something for you, Revere. General Howe said Warren's death was worth five hundred men to him."

The British had 1,100 casualties. They still occupied Charlestown. But it was agreed, in the days that followed, that the victory had been ours. With not enough powder, we'd inflicted serious losses on them. The army Warren had assembled had held.

But Warren was dead. Gone. For days after, Father went about the house silent. And Rachel was teary-eyed.

I was numb. I went about, bumping into things, staring into the air. I scarcely ate. I didn't hear people when they spoke to me.

Nobody noticed. For which I was gratified.

WE WENT ON.

That summer Doctor Church was found guilty in a court-martial of "holding criminal correspondence with the enemy."

Now Father and Rachel knew what had happened to the letter and money she sent with him. Likely, he'd turned it over to General Gage, like so much of the information he'd been selling to Gage all along from the Provincial Congress.

He was sent to prison in Connecticut. In the fall he was sent off on a ship to the West Indies.

A man named Washington came to Cambridge that summer to set up headquarters and take over the army that Warren had assembled.

Washington stopped in Watertown one July day, on his way to take command. We all went out to see him. Grandmother said he looked like an uppity Virginian. But I liked the looks of him. He was very tall and distinguished.

In November, Rachel told us she was in circumstances. We stayed the winter in Watertown. In the spring, at the end of March, we went back to Boston.

General Gage and his troops had left on the seventeenth. On the fifth, six years to the day after the Boston Massacre, Washington took possession of Dorchester Heights. He posted his big cannon there, the ones Henry Knox had brought down from Ticonderoga and Crown Point that winter in the snow, pulled by herds of oxen.

Boston under the British was near destroyed and disease-ridden. We came back to find Old North Meeting torn down. The British needed the ground for drilling and the church itself for firewood.

There were earthworks on the Common. All the trees had been cut down for firewood. The steeple of West Street Church was gone. Old South had no more pews. It had been gutted. It was filled with dirt the British had carted in to make the place a riding ring for the Queen's Light Dragoons.

Many Rebel houses were ruined. Ours still stood. Paul took care of it and Father's shop.

A few weeks after Father rode back in with other Whig leaders, we arrived.

We had a joyous reunion with Paul, who was taller than Father now and had many stories to tell us.

Some old friends who had been Tories were gone. Lady Frankland for one. She'd turned her house over to her brother and was gone to Halifax. With the Saltonstalls, the Olivers, the Sewalls, Clarks, and Mathers.

All the Episcopal ministers were gone. As

were many merchants, tradesmen, and mechanics.

Amos Lincoln was still there. Waiting for Debby.

The first thing Father did was ask to join the army. He wanted a field command. They did not give it to him. But none other than General Washington asked him to go to Castle Island to repair the damage the British had done to the fortifications there. The cannon were in need of fixing.

Father was commissioned major in a special regiment raised for the defense of Boston. He took Paul with him as his lieutenant.

In April, they had a funeral for Doctor Warren in Boston. But first they had to go and bring him down from the hill. Where he'd gone that day with a sprig of a flower in his buttonhole and a book of poetry in his pocket.

DOCTOR WARREN'S two younger brothers asked Father to row over to Charlestown to bring home Doctor Warren. A sexton friend went with them.

I wanted to go, but Father wouldn't let me.

So I waited on the shore in the same spot I'd

waited for Father to return that night they kept him prisoner on Castle Island. It was the least I could do for Doctor Warren.

They were gone all afternoon. When they came back, when they'd waded ashore, pulling the boat, I saw the shroud-covered thing inside it.

Father came toward me. "Have you been waiting all this time?"

"Did you find him?"

"Yes. I had to identify him."

"Could you?"

"Yes, by the teeth I put in his mouth last year."

"Oh."

"And by this." He took something out of his pocket. I could scarce recognize it at first. It seemed to be a book. It was dusty and the binding was loose.

And then I did recognize it. And I could barely see it for the tears that blinded my eyes.

It was the book of poetry I'd given him the day he left for the hill. "It was in his pocket," Father said. "Wasn't this once yours, Sarah?"

"Yes, I gave it to him," I said.

He said nothing. But he patted me on the shoulder. That said all.

THE FUNERAL for Warren was as grand as any in Boston, a town that puts on grand funerals.

The procession was long; the Masons came out in full force. Doctor Cooper prayed over him. A Mason gave an eloquent oration that Warren would be proud of.

I sat in King's Chapel with Rachel and Debby and the children, but I did not hear the oration.

I heard Doctor Warren's voice, as it was when he came to me in my room that night when we quarreled. And he picked up the book of poetry.

No longer mourn for me when I am dead, than you shall hear the surly sullen bell, give warning to the world that I am fled, from this vile world, with vilest worms to dwell. Nay, if you read this line, remember not, the hand that writ it, for I love you so, that I in your sweet thoughts would be forgot, if thinking on me then should make you woe.

And when I was not hearing those words, I was thinking how he'd turned to me at the gate that day and formed some other words.

Were they "I forgive you, Sarah?"

I don't know. They were drowned out by the cannon.

But I do know this. Father thinks he has a secret. So does Rachel. So, for that matter, did Doctor Warren.

He was determined to take his, about his informer, to the grave with him.

Who fired the first shot at Lexington? Does it matter?

Who informed Doctor Warren that General Gage was going to march on Concord? Does it matter?

Who brought Margaret Gage to Doctor Warren in the first place? Does it matter?

The war was in the making for years. Someone would have done all of these things, sooner or later.

So it seems I am the only one to *really* have a secret. Mine is not half so grand as the others. Mine is shabby and sad.

I had a quarrel with Doctor Warren. That in itself is not bad. What is bad is that I let the time pass for settling it.

I let the words go unsaid. Until it was too late.

Even though I shouted the words to him, it was too late. They were drowned out by the cannon. As were his to me.

I did not make it up with a dear friend before he died. And that is all that matters in the end.

What matters, Father? What's true? Or what people think?

What's true, Sarah, he would say.

And what's true is that I shall carry my shabby, sad secret with me forever. To the grave.

IN JUNE, Rachel was brought to bed of a child. A boy child. They named him John after my father's brother, who had died during the siege of Boston.

The baby died in a month.

In December, Rachel told us she was in circumstances again. In July of 1777, Joseph Warren Revere was born. I shall teach my little brother well. And one of the things I shall teach him is that you must always make it up with a dear friend when you have a quarrel. Before it is too late.

And if Joseph Warren Revere refuses to believe me about this, then mayhap, just mayhap, I may have to tell him my secret. We'll see.

Author's Note

*H*ISTORY IS MADE UP of people. This is the truth that motivates historical novelists. Great battles, political upheavals, courageous and dastardly acts are all the outpourings of human souls who have everyday problems, hopes, afflictions, and dreams. And who are influenced by the social dictums of their times.

Three things I discovered about Paul Revere in doing research made me want to write this book.

One, he had sixteen children. (Lucy, Harriet, a second John, Maria, and a third John were born after the time period of this book.)

Two, he took many rides before his famous one.

Three, the deposition he wrote for the Whig leaders was suppressed in the aftermath of the battles of Lexington and Concord. Why? Likely because Revere refused to testify that the "Regulars" (British) fired the first shot at Lexington.

All these facts heightened his humanity for me. The last discovery posed a great, unanswered mystery. Did Paul Revere go to his grave knowing who fired the first shot at Lexington?

It was enough to set me off to do more research to see what I could discover and to embark on a book. Because writing, in itself, is a process of discovery.

What I found was that the Paul Revere I'd known had been trivialized into almost a cartoon character. But this is not unusual. Americans do this with all the founding fathers. Why, I do not know. Is it because the only really intense study of the American Revolution is done in grade school? At a time when all heroes come across as myth and legend, on a par with the current rage in television superheroes?

I do know this: the real truth about our founding fathers is eye-opening. But, for all my academic reading, I knew the interpretation of the facts would be up to me.

History will not tell us, for instance, if Rachel, Paul's second wife, knew of his involvement in subversive activities against the Crown. It will not tell us how his children felt about his being away from home so much. Or what the relationships of the children were to each other and to Rachel.

We know Paul's mother lived with them. But what kind of a grandmother was she? Were any of the children disfigured with scars from the pox? We can only speculate.

Doctor Joseph Warren, probably the most overlooked figure in Revolutionary War history, was a close friend of Revere's, close enough for Revere to help retrieve his body from "the hill" and bring it back to Boston for burial after the British evacuated that town.

Sarah Revere was thirteen at the time of her father's famous ride. Doctor Warren was young, just thirty-four, ofttimes cited as one of the most handsome men in Boston, and a widower. No, history doesn't tell us that Sarah was smitten with him. The conclusions I draw in my book about this and Rachel's friendship with Warren are just that. My conclusions.

However, I never strayed from the historical facts.

The Reverend William Gordon did write and publish an article about Revere's famous ride by June of 1775, two months after the event. Gordon interviewed, for background, as many participants in the Battle of Lexington as he could.

Revere did make teeth for Doctor Warren that spring and did identify Warren's body on the hill by the teeth he wired in, perhaps the first American dentist ever to perform such a grisly service.

Warren, the levelheaded intellectual who worked behind the scenes, with his house in Boston as Whig headquarters in those last dangerous days before Lexington, did summon Revere, at just the right moment, to take his famous ride.

The horse ridden was named Brown Beauty.

Warren went on to orchestrate things with the Massachusetts Committee of Safety right after Lexington, then rushed off to lead the Yankee militia as they stood against the British that day, attacking as the British retreated back to Boston.

Then, at Hastings House in Cambridge, sitting with the Committee of Safety, he drafted the petition to assemble the army. And it came into being, with no real military leadership. In a day when everything our president does is open to media-sniping, when politicians don't act without the certainty of personal gain, Warren put himself on the line in many ways. His influence brought order out of the confusion and chaos that followed Lexington.

He wrote another letter to the "Inhabitants of Great Britain." The committee rushed it to England, along with nearly one hundred depositions taken from those who had fought at Lexington and Concord, aboard the very fast schooner *Quero,* owned by Captain John Derby of Salem. And news of the event reached Parliament before the British dispatches, gaining the Americans the advantage of positive public opinion in Great Britain.

Having been responsible for assembling the army, Warren went to fight in the battle of Breed's Hill exactly as I described, with a headache from wine and no sleep. He was dressed as I described, as if for a frolic, and with a book of poetry in his pocket. He had no uniform. Colonel William Prescott offered him the command, but no, he was not yet ready to assume rank.

On the afternoon of April 18, 1775, as he received reports that the British Regulars were about to make a move that had long been expected, Doctor Warren "applied to the person who had been retained, and got intelligence of their whole design."

Was that person he retained Margaret Kemble Gage, the American wife of Sir William Gage, the British commander? Many historians think so. But we shall never know, for sure. Doctor Warren took his secret to the grave.

He fought and died as he lived, a responsible, caring citizen, killed in that "foolish endeavor," the battle known as Bunker Hill (really Breed's Hill), which was our baptism as a nation.

What of Lady Frankland? The story of how Sir Henry Frankland, Collector of the Port of Boston, came upon Agnes Surriage, a barefoot serving girl scrubbing floors in a New England inn, subsequently brought her to his gracious Boston home to educate her, then married her, is the stuff of New England folklore. She was Lady Frankland at the time of this story, living in Boston as a Tory. Her role in the book is of my own making.

For the record: The letter Rachel penned to her husband from Boston right after the Battle of Lexington never got to him. Nor did the hundred twenty-five pounds. Doctor Church, the traitor, gave it to General Gage, and the letter turned up in Gage's private papers two centuries later. But not the money.

Mary Revere (Second Mary in the book), who was seven at the time and whom I created as fearful of dying, lived until 1853. Of all the daughters of Revere's first wife, she lived the longest. She married Jedidiah Lincoln, and they had seven children.

Debby (Deborah) married Amos Lincoln. They had nine children, and she died in 1797.

Sarah, my narrator, married John Bradford. There is no record of any children. She died in 1791.

Elizabeth married Amos Lincoln after her sister Debby died. They had five children, and she died in 1805. (His fourth cousin, Thomas Lincoln of Virginia, had not yet married Nancy Hanks, but when they did, their son would be named Abraham.)

Young Paul became a silversmith and married Sally Edwards. They had twelve children.

Frances married Thomas Stevens Eayres, a silversmith. They had five children.

Joshua became a merchant, in business with his father, and died in 1801.

Joseph Warren Revere took over the copper business from his father in 1810. He married Mary Robbins, and they had eight children.

Rachel died in 1813, Paul in 1818, both after the War of 1812. From Paul Revere's mill in Canton came the copper sheets used for the hull of the U.S.S. *Constitution*.

In all, Paul had fifty-one grandchildren. One, John Revere, became president of the Revere Copper Company. Another, Edward Hutchinson Revere, served in the 20th Massachusetts Regiment in the Civil War and was killed at Antietam. Still another, Paul Joseph Revere, also served in the same regiment and died of wounds he received at Gettysburg. Grandson Joseph Warren Revere became a brigadier general of Union troops.

Paul Revere's house stands today, in Boston, open to the public.

His manner of saying, in my book, "What's acting?" and calling his children "my lambs" are taken directly from history.

—Ann Rinaldi

Bibliography

Drake, Samuel Adams. *New England Legends & Folk Lore.* Secaucus, NJ: Castle Books, 1993.

Fischer, David Hackett. *Paul Revere's Ride.* New York: Oxford University Press, 1994.

Forbes, Esther. *Paul Revere and the World He Lived In.* Boston: Houghton Mifflin Company, 1942.

Massachusetts Historical Society. *Paul Revere: Three Accounts of his Famous Ride.* Portland, ME: Anthoensen Press, 1976.

Moreno, Edgard, Patrick Leehey, M. Skerry, E. Janine, Deborah Federhen, A. Steblecki, J. Edity (Contributing Authors). *Paul Revere—Artisan, Businessman, and Patriot: The Man Behind the Myth.* Boston: The Paul Revere Memorial Association, 1988.

Norton, Mary Beth. *Liberty's Daughters: The Revolutionary Experience of American Women, 1750–1800.* Boston: Little, Brown and Company, 1980.

Sprigg, June. *Domestick Beings.* New York: Alfred A. Knopf, 1984.

Tourtellot, Arthur B. *Lexington and Concord: The Beginning of the War of the American Revolution.* New York: W. W. Norton & Company, 1959.

Trevelyan, George Otto. *The American Revolution.* New York: David McKay Company, Inc., 1899.

Other titles now available:

*Look for exciting new titles to come in the
Great Episodes series of historical fiction.*